Welcome to [handwritten, illegible]!

GRIMM UP NORTH

DAVID J. GATWARD

WEIRDSTONE PUBLISHING

Grimm Up North
By
David J. Gatward

Copyright © 2020 by David J. Gatward
All rights reserved.

To Barry, Gordon, and Jon,
for being mad enough to persuade me
to write crime fiction in the first place.
Here on in, I blame you.

And for Wayne 'Scoff' Winspear and Phil Guy.

Grimm: nickname for a dour and forbidding individual, from Old High German grim [meaning] 'stern', 'severe'. From a Germanic personal name, Grima, [meaning] 'mask'. (*www.ancestory.co.uk*)

CHAPTER ONE

A TWO-WORD TEXT MESSAGE CHANGED FIFTEEN-YEAR-old Sophie Hodgson's life for good, but not for the better, not by a long shot. And in retrospect, she knew that she probably shouldn't have sent it, or at the very least had a plan to deal with the veritable shit storm which followed. But send it she did and plan she didn't. Such is the lot of a teenage girl.

It had been one of those weeks, or at least it had been for Sophie. The kind of week where the world decides to not so much rain on your parade, as to relieve itself on your cornflakes in the morning and then, just for good measure, defecate on your pillow when you go to bed.

It was June, and a hot one at that. And Wensleydale, where Sophie had lived her whole life, was basking not just in the sunshine, but the extra money rolling in from all of the tourists clogging up the roads just to take photos of it.

For any normal teenage girl, such weather would've meant a weekend hanging around in the park with mates in the sunshine, drinking booze nicked from someone's parents' fridge, and hopefully getting off with a fit boy from the year above. Not for Sophie though. No. Because the world was being an absolute bastard.

It had all started to go wrong on Sunday, courtesy of the two-word text message she had decided to send in the middle of the morning service at church. She'd thought about talking to her mum about it first, but what was the point? And her dad was just too weak to do anything about it anyway. So, in the middle of a rather extensive prayer session, she typed *I KNOW* and hit 'send'. A couple of minutes later, Sophie's phone had buzzed, and she'd stared down at the screen on her phone to read the reply: *I HAVE NO IDEA WHAT YOU ARE TALKING ABOUT*. Her reaction to this message only added to her troubles, because apparently church wasn't the kind of place where people who had just received an unwanted message were allowed to stand up and shout out, 'You lying bastard!'

Sophie's parents, especially her mum, would have found it difficult enough to deal with hearing their precious daughter using such language at all, but in church? Well, their horror and disgust had been immediately clear. Dragged out of the building, with the prayers still in session, and thrown into the back of their car, Sophie's mum had driven them home at a terrifying speed, treating the road back up the dale like a rally course, all the while raging at her, because surely Sophie knew better than to behave like that, and where on earth did she learn such language anyway?

Sent to her room, Sophie was told in no uncertain terms that not only was she grounded for a month, but that she had lost all mobile phone privileges. Her mum had even gone so far as to lock the phone away in her little safe. A shame for her then that Sophie had known the combination for the lock for years.

The rest of Sunday had been a bright and vibrant mix of: Sophie playing her music too loud and being shouted at by her mum to turn it down, because it was giving her father another one of his migraines; Sophie throwing things around her bedroom and being shouted at by her mum to have some respect for their beautiful house; Sophie refusing to come down for dinner in the evening and being shouted at by her mum for, well, refusing to come down for dinner in the evening.

When Monday arrived, the week had clearly decided to regard Sunday's debacle as a challenge it could not only meet, but crush. And so, on arrival at school, Sophie had quickly discovered to her delight that a certain group of girls, whom she had nothing in common with and did her best to avoid, had come up with a new and completely hilarious name for her. It was something they did a lot, mainly because they had decided in year seven that Sophie going to church with her parents every week was the weirdest, saddest thing they'd ever heard of. And from that point onwards, their mission had been to make her life, if not completely unbearable, certainly less fun whenever they pushed their way into it. It was a girl called Jennifer Sharp who shouted it out first when Sophie had arrived at school, and the words, 'Hey look! Here comes Celibate Sophie!' not only embarrassed her, but made her blood boil.

Sophie's response had shocked everyone, not least herself, because she wasn't a violent person. With Jennifer still laughing, Sophie had walked right up to her and slapped her across the side of the head so hard that the girl had dropped like liquid, crashing down onto her knees with a scream. After a meeting with the head teacher, a woman called Mrs Stevens, who only ever wore black and was approximately the size of a blue whale, Sophie had been suspended for the rest of the day and sent home, a meeting arranged for the following morning with the head teacher, Sophie, and her mum.

The suspension only added to the troubles at home, with her mum moving from abject rage to pure silence. And then, to add vinegar and salt to the already seeping wound of her life, Sophie was banned from seeing her boyfriend until the summer holidays, because that was, in her mum's words, 'just another distraction' from her considerably more important school work. And by now, the thing which had started it all, that two-word text, well Sophie just didn't care anymore. There was just no point in the end, was there? No one listened, no one cared. And she'd had enough of the lies. So, when Wednesday morning came around, the only thing she could think to do was to run. So that's what she did. She *ran* . . .

Sophie knew that running away wouldn't solve anything, indeed there was every chance it would only make things worse. But she didn't care because if all it did was punish her mum and make her, just for once, actually *listen*, then it was worth it. She had no idea where she was going to go, or for how long, just that she needed to get the hell away for a day or two. She had enough money in her account, would pack a few things, and then just sod off to anywhere that wasn't *here*. She was fifteen, but she looked older, and was fairly sure she could find somewhere cheap to bed down for a night or two. She wouldn't even tell her boyfriend because that just wasn't fair on him.

With her school bag packed with some spare clothes and

a load of snacks from the kitchen, her phone from her mother's safe, and a quick raid of the petty cash pot on the mantelpiece in the lounge, Sophie headed off to catch the school bus. And an hour later, when everyone got off to walk down the steps into the school, Sophie turned around and headed into town.

At first, the idea had seemed brilliant. Those first few steps away from the school had been ones walked on clouds. Sophie had breathed freedom in the air and after a quick change in the public toilets jumped on a bus to Harrogate.

The day was a total blast and Sophie soaked up the freedom of it, the sense of release. No one knew where she was, and she could do as she pleased. So that's exactly what she did, spending the hours shopping, eating junk food, and soaking up the sun in a park.

When evening came around, Sophie decided it was probably best that she find somewhere to sleep for the night. So, she jumped online and found a backpackers' hostel, but when she went to try and book, she couldn't find her wallet, and that didn't just have her money, but her bank card as well.

With no money or access to any, and thus no other option, Sophie found herself in the arse end of nowhere, not wanting to go home and yet now desperate to do just that. And that meant trying to hitch a ride. Yes, she could have just called her parents, but there was no way that Sophie was going to give them the satisfaction of her failure. No way at all. So, she would be making her own way home, thank you very much.

After an hour of heading out of town, walking in the direction of home, Sophie had come very close to giving in, when a small blue van had pulled over and the driver had offered her a lift. Sophie had opened the door and been about to climb in when a hand had grabbed her arm and spun her around, a shout scaring the driver enough to have him race off.

Shocked that anyone would do such a thing, Sophie had opened her mouth to scream abuse, only to find eyes she recognised staring back at her, and the only real thought in her mind at that moment being that perhaps, sending that two-word text a few days ago hadn't been such a good idea after all.

CHAPTER TWO

Detective Chief Inspector Harry Grimm had a face on him that would shame a pug, if that pug had first been half beaten to death with a cricket bat and then chewed on enthusiastically by a hippo. It was a face he wore particularly well, crafted from wounds he'd sustained from an IED when he was in the Parachute Regiment, and then honed over the years into something just short of being hard and horrible enough to make a grown man shit himself. It wasn't just about looking angry, it was more about really giving the other person the impression that at any point soon he was going to reach out, rip their face off, then eat it. The fact that he buzz-cut his own hair at grade 1 length only added to his imposing visage, and that was just the way he liked it. Right now, though, Harry was doing his best to smooth out the lines in his face a bit and take it down a notch from 'serial killer' to something that wasn't that, which wasn't easy to do, not least because a lot of the lines were scars, and also because it was sat as it was on top of his imposing frame. Okay, so he wasn't a six-foot-six Jack Reacher by any stretch of the imagination, but at six-foot-three, and with broad shoulders still hefty with muscle, he could still, and with considerable ease, strike the fear of God into most. Which was something he rather enjoyed.

It was Saturday afternoon and Harry was reclining at a round table in a small room with a tall man in a smart suit. His own attire was the kind generally found in the bargain section of a charity shop. Not that he'd bought any of it from one himself, but he figured it would be where it would end up eventually. This was Bristol after all, and if there was anywhere on earth more into labelling everything second-hand and a bit shit as 'vintage' then he'd be very surprised. Some of the charity shops he'd seen somehow made you feel under-dressed. Hipsters had a lot to answer for.

'So,' the tall man said, adjusting his tie then nodding conspiratorially, 'we have a deal, yes?'

Harry was fighting every instinct in his body to not just reach across the table, grab the man by the neck, and smash his tidy, smug face off the varnished wood between them. There was something unique about the sound of a skull smacking off stained pine, a sort of wet hollow sound which had a ring to it. And after that, rub it into the wall at his side, really grind it in there to make sure there wasn't much left at the end other than mince.

Regardless of the well-dressed businessman image the man was trying to pull off, they both knew that underneath it all, he was little more than gold-plated scum. And it was Harry's job to make the scum of the world pay, which he did rather well, though perhaps with a little too much enthusiasm at times.

'Yes,' Harry said, 'we do.'

'Good,' the tall man said. 'And the delivery is all arranged? The package undamaged?'

Those words, 'package undamaged', forced bile to rise into Harry's throat. He had to stay calm, had to make sure he didn't do anything he'd regret. If he buggered this up now then that was months of undercover work down the drain, but this man . . . *this thing*. . .

'As agreed,' Harry said, refusing to use the same words, because the package was a supposed thirteen-year-old girl, and because undamaged meant that the person this scumbag worked for, *procured* for, would only take the bait if he was sure that she was a virgin. A thirteen-year-old girl! How was her virginity even to be considered a thing at all? Sometimes Harry found himself hating the world, but above all, he hated people the most, because so many of them, it seemed, like this fetid piss stain of a man in front of him, were complete and utter bastards.

The tall man stood up and reached out a hand for Harry to shake. He took it, imagining just what it would feel like to crush it, then use it to rip the arm off at the shoulder. It would feel good, Harry decided, while trying to make his smile convincing, no it would feel better than good. It would feel absolutely bloody fantastic.

'Nice doing business with you,' the tall man said. 'Half the money will be transferred now, the rest on delivery.'

The tall man turned his phone around so that Harry could see the screen and the details of the transaction being completed there and then.

And that was it. That was all Harry had needed. Confirmation that money had exchanged hands, that the deal had been done, that money had been exchanged for services rendered. Now, all he had to do was let the rest of the team know so that they could swoop in and make this stain of a man's life take a nosedive into the rotting, stinking hell he so deserved. There were plenty of people on the inside, locked up and bored, who would certainly see to that, of that, Harry was absolutely sure. And boy oh boy was he going to enjoy watching it happen.

The operation had been some time in the making. Human trafficking, slavery, it was more common than the average Joe Public would ever care to know. And the sex trade was the murkier side of something already so filthy that every time Harry was involved, he wanted to just hose himself down with industrial-strength disinfectant. This, however, had been different; rumours of high bidders, hiding behind numerous security and defence systems, spending money on a new plaything. Harry's job had been to pose as someone who could offer what they were after, which he'd done, and now it was time to bring it home. The thirteen-year-old girl wasn't real. None of it was. But it was convincing enough and had hooked them a prize catch. Just a pity that there were so many others out there swimming around in the depths.

As the tall man made to leave the room, Harry stood up and coughed. But it wasn't an 'I've got a tickly throat' cough, or even an 'I just swallowed a fly' cough. No. This was a cough that demanded absolutely, undivided attention.

The tall man turned around, frustration bristling in his movement. 'Yes? What is it?'

'This,' Harry said, and pulled his police ID from his pocket.

The tall man didn't flinch.

This surprised Harry and twisted his gut a little. But he carried on anyway because that was what Harry was like. Backing out just wasn't an option, an attitude he'd always had and one which had been finely tuned in the Paras.

'Now, before we get to all that *I'm arresting you on suspicion of* bollocks,' Harry said, 'I'd like you to have a look at something, if that's okay? Though, don't go confusing that with me asking your permission or anything. I'm telling you it's okay. Okay?'

The tall man was now smiling, Harry noticed. And no one smiled when they were being arrested. No one. Yes, some of the harder bastards would swear at you, spit at you, tell you they were going to kill you and your family, and your family's dog, but they never smiled. That was just weird. *This* was weird. Harry didn't like it.

Harry pulled out a folded piece of card from a trouser pocket. 'This is a photograph,' he said, unfolding it. 'I know that I'm stating the blatantly bloody obvious here, but I like to make things nice and clear. You know, like the fact that you and that total bastard you work for will be going to prison for a very long time indeed and not one day of it will be pleasant, for numerous reasons, which I'll let your imagination conjure up for now. But anyway, this photograph here: do you recognise the man in it?'

The tall man didn't even bother looking at the photograph in Harry's hand. He was just too damned busy smiling. It was the kind of smile Harry wanted to rip off, the sound of it like sticky tape being pulled.

'The photograph,' Harry said, holding it a bit higher, to give the man a really good look. 'Could you just have a look? I know it's old and faded, but you can clearly make out what he looks like. I mean, he's a lot older now, but he won't look much different, I'm sure. Once a bastard, always a bastard, right? He's into the same stuff as you, if you know what I mean.'

And still, the man just smiled.

'You're smiling,' Harry said, giving up on the photograph and stuffing it back into his pocket. 'Why are you smiling? I'm arresting you and you're smiling. Why? Are you having fun? Is something funny? Is it my hair? It usually is. I do it myself, you see, buzz cut it at home, to save a few quid. Means I sometimes miss bits. Is there a tuft? I bet there's a tuft.'

This in itself was funny, Harry thought, because if he was honest—and he really did try to be most of the time—then it was never his hair that people stared at. Not when there was so much else there to bedazzle the eyes with thanks to the IED which had done its best to remove the left side of his face. He was ugly, wore a face that had the uncanny resemblance to meat that was chewed and spat out by a wolf. People stared and he was used to it. People even flinched sometimes. Yet it was also a shield and Harry could hide behind the face, take cover behind his very own grim façade.

The tall man continued to smile and then Harry heard a click from behind him. It was the click of a door latch, the only problem with that was that Harry knew there was no door behind him. Or at least he thought he did, until now, thanks to that sound. It was just a flat wall in a small room in a nondescript warehouse on the outskirts of town. The room had just one door, the one he'd entered through, the one the tall man was now standing in.

Rough hands grabbed Harry and something thin and biting dropped over his neck and yanked him back.

Shit . . .

The man's smile slipped from his face like ice from a hot

tin roof. 'Before we part,' he said, his voice greasy smooth, 'how is it that you ended up looking . . .' He paused and glanced upwards, as though the corner of the room would be able to help him with exactly what he was trying to say. 'I mean, you have to look at that, your *face*, every day. How can you stand it?'

Harry was choking and hoping the cavalry would arrive soon or he would pass out.

'Were you in a car accident? Is that it?'

Harry briefly imagined the device which had nearly killed him being rammed up the arse of this wank stain and then exploding, shredding him in a cartoonish display of fleshy ribbons and pink mist. Then his world went dark as a black cotton bag, which stunk of blood and vomit, was dropped over his head and cinched at his neck. At the same time, something hard crashed into the back of his legs, dropping him to the floor, only he didn't make it that far, because whoever had thrust the bag over his head was now using it to hold him up on his feet. Nice touch.

Harry coughed and choked, struggling against the bag, his arms thrashing and legs kicking, then something was clamped over his mouth as a thick arm wrapped itself around his neck. Chloroform, Harry noticed almost with interest, before he sagged and blacked out.

Harry came to in the back of a van. He was alone, his head hurt like hell, and he was also getting a little peckish. But food would have to wait. Right now, he was properly in the shit, right up to the eyeballs, because if everything had gone according to plan then this was not where he should have been. He should've been back at the station with the rest of the team, celebrating with some actual real coffee that they saved for special occasions. There would've been pastries, too, because that's what he always bought when something went well. And the fact that he'd brought the photograph out again would've been forgotten very quickly indeed. He hadn't done it in months so, no damage done. But none of this was what Harry, or anyone, would have ever described as going well. And as for the photograph? He was really in for it this time, of that he had no doubt at all.

Harry sat up, which wasn't easy with his wrists tied behind his back. He knocked against something and heard the thump of it falling or tumbling. He could smell concrete as well, then as he shuffled to his right. With a quick bit of deduction, which included grabbing stuff with his hands and trying to imagine what it was like he was a contestant on a particularly cheap and nasty game show, Harry realised he was in a builder's van. And that gave him an idea. He wasn't about to A-Team the shit out of whatever was with him in the darkness, and spring out of the rear door with a flamethrower and a potato cannon, but he was pretty sure that the rough edge of a brick would be able to wear through the plastic tag that had been used on his wrists, assuming he still had enough time . . .

THE TWO MEN in the front of the van pulled the vehicle off the main road and headed off down a track. It was a bumpy ride and they both laughed at the thought of their passenger unconscious and tied up in the back and how he was getting knocked about.

At the end of the track, they pulled the van into an old quarry which contained a small and very deep pool, and a rough-looking shed. They had been here a number of other times over the years and the task ahead was just another day at the office for them, if that office was a place where you could easily dispose of someone in a tub of acid before shipping said tub out into the Bristol Channel to be emptied of its contents.

With the engine switched off, they both exited the van, and one of them headed over to the shed to get things set up, while the other strode round to the back doors. He was armed with a revolver, they both were, but he soon realised he couldn't open the back door if he was carrying it in one hand, because the door was too stiff, and really, hadn't this happened last time? He'd need to oil it. Or get someone else to do it. Yeah, that was probably the better option. And so, gripping the weapon under his arm for a moment, he reached down to the door handle and gave it a hard yank.

The doors burst open as though they'd been holding back flood water, sending the man skipping backwards. He stumbled, dazed for a second by what had just happened, his vision filled with the shape of something launching itself from out of the darkness lurking inside the van. It crashed into him, knocking his pistol away and onto the ground, then drove him into the dirt. God, the weight of it was crushing his chest and he couldn't breathe and there was dust in his eyes, up his nose, in his mouth! Then, as he struggled against the thing, this monstrous awful thing, it growled at him and drove its forehead into his face, destroying his nose, before he was tumbled over onto his chest, his arms yanked painfully upwards and his wrists tied together.

Harry leaned down into the ear of the man beneath him. 'Just so you know, I'm not a fan of everything that's just happened to me. Not by a country mile, pal. And that broken nose you've got? See it as a warning shot across your bow. If you try anything else, and I mean anything at all, because right now even blinking is going to push me over the edge, then you'll be shitting out teeth for the rest of the week, that I promise.' He heaved the man to his feet. 'Now, let's put you somewhere more comfortable, shall we?'

With probably a little bit too much force, Harry threw the man into the back of his own van.

'You're police!' the man cried back at him as Harry stared into the dark interior. 'You can't do this! I'll have you! I'll sue!'

'I didn't do anything, pal,' Harry said. 'Not a thing.' Then he slammed the door shut.

It was then that the crack of a weapon being fired broke into the moment and Harry dived for cover.

CHAPTER THREE

It wasn't the first time Harry had been shot at by any stretch of the imagination. In many ways, it was a sound he was actually very accustomed to. He was even unlucky enough to know what it was like to be hit, not just once, but on rather too many occasions. Though taking shrapnel to the face had been the worst, if only because of what it had left behind, or not, as was actually the case, considering how much of his face the IED had destroyed. The scarring was, as someone he'd arrested one night after a brawl in a pub had pointed out, 'epic', and he'd got off lightly really, all things considered. At least he could still see through both eyes, which was more than could be said for a lot of lads who had suffered worse. It wasn't something that happened as often as it once had, people commenting on it, and Harry was very thankful for that.

Being a police officer, even working undercover, didn't come with as much live fire being thrown his way as it had when he'd been in the Paras. But then, Harry had seen tours in Iraq and Afghanistan and a good number of other places, too, and there was no avoiding it in places like that. Sometimes it filled the air like flies. He'd been a lot younger then, angrier too, if that could be believed, but that world was a long time ago now, a very long time indeed. And yet, deep down, the Para was still alive, and the soldier he had been came to life at the sound of those rounds coming in.

Harry raced for cover behind the van, looking for anything he could use as a weapon. Not a problem when he'd been a Para, but now, very much so. He spotted the pistol that had been carried by the bloke he'd just thrown into the van. The temptation was there to use it, but even from where he was standing, he could see that to do so would be as much a risk to himself as anyone else. It was, as with so many illegal guns on the streets, a blank firer repurposed to take live rounds. What idiot would ever trust something like that? thought Harry. It didn't matter anyway, because he was fine with the police not carrying weapons, always had been, because the damned things were more dangerous than most people had any clue about. Though sometimes he did find himself wondering if it would swing things in their favour a little now and again.

A shout rang out and was answered by more shouting from inside the van, which was mainly swearing and abuse, but Harry wasn't listening.

So that was two, Harry noted. And if both men were carrying similar weapons, that meant there were four rounds left, assuming of course that he wasn't reloading as he went.

Harry edged along the side of the van towards the front to see if he could get eyes on the other man. As he went to sneak a peek through the windows another shot rang out, crashing through the glass. Too close . . .

Harry dropped to the ground and had a look under the

van. He could see feet approaching now, just a couple of metres away on the other side from him. He also spotted a stick which would come in useful and he quickly and quietly grabbed it.

Keeping himself low, Harry edged forwards, under the now smashed window in the driver's door, until he was at the front of the van. Then he grabbed a few stones and lobbed them back around to the rear from where he had just come.

Harry heard footsteps hurrying to where he'd thrown the stones. With a deep breath, he slid forward, still low, around the front of the van and then back down the other side, the stick held ready.

'Where are you, you ugly bastard?' a voice called out, the words spitting into the air through clenched teeth.

Harry answered with actions instead of words, whipping himself around the rear offside corner of the van to bring the stick around in a wide, violent arc to connect with the man's right arm. The screech of agony he released set a few pigeons into flight from some nearby trees. Harry brought the stick in again, this time slamming it down hard onto the hand holding the pistol. The man dropped it with another roar of pain, only to have it muffled with the van door as Harry grabbed him and slammed him into it like he was trying to make him eat it, hooking his right arm up his spine, and gripping his hand in a nice little hold meant that any struggling on the part of the kidnapping bastard in front of him would potentially result in the thumb being dislocated.

Harry was breathing heavily. Once upon a time, he'd have been able to hammer out a five-kilometre run in less than twenty minutes easily. Now though, not so much. But he was still fairly fit, and right now, he had more than enough in the tank to keep these two arseholes pinned until help arrived.

With a quick search of the man's pockets, Harry found a phone. He then used the thumb he was holding to open it. Fingerprint recognition wasn't something he had on his own phone, for just this reason: it was way easier to break than a code.

Harry punched in a number and waited for the answer.

'If this is who I think it is, then you are so deep in the shit right now that you won't just need armbands, you'll need a bloody snorkel!'

There was definitely something about her tone which made Harry suspect he may have gone a bit too far this time. Perhaps it was the volume, perhaps it was the swearing, or perhaps it was the fact that Detective Superintendent Alice Firbank rarely, if ever, did either of those things unless someone was about to have the world fall on their head. At which point, she could become rather creative with both.

'I've got them,' Harry said. 'I'll send you a location in a sec.'

'Got them?' came the reply, the voice displaying barely controlled rage. 'And you say that like this was all planned from the beginning! Was it planned, Harry? Was it? No, I don't think it was, do you?'

'There was another door,' Harry said, attempting to explain.

'We know there was another door!' the Detective Superintendent snapped, biting the end off what Harry was saying and chewing it down like a rich tea biscuit. 'How else would they have got in, hmm? But then they probably wouldn't have needed to, would they, if you hadn't shown that damned photograph!'

Yeah, he'd gone a bit too far, but he was getting annoyed now, and that was never good. 'Why did no one come in, Ma'am?' Harry asked. 'Where was everyone when I was getting hauled out on my arse?'

Silence for a moment from the other end, which was almost worse.

'You want to try that again, Grimm? Or are you seriously going to try and blame everyone else for this monumental shitstorm?'

She had a point, Harry thought, but then she always did, didn't she?

'Look, I've got them –'

'And that's supposed to make everything better, is it?' the voice on the other end asked, jumping in once again before he'd finished. 'Two pawns do not make up for a king, and you know that as well as I. What were you thinking, Harry? Why not wait until we had the bastard down at the station and in an interview room and do it then?'

Harry didn't have an answer. He really, truly didn't. But then he'd not had an answer for years, had he? Because that photo was the only reason he'd joined the force in the first place. Well, the person in it was, at any rate.

The arsehole between himself and the van was squirming. Harry looked at the phone in his hand and, in a moment of pure madness, killed the call. That was something else which would come back and bite him, but in for a penny, he thought. He scrolled back through recent calls. And there it was. Harry clicked on the number and held the phone back up next to his ear.

'Is he dealt with?'

Harry would recognise that slimy voice anywhere. 'No, I'm not,' he said. 'So, what say we make a deal?'

Harry heard the deepest of breaths and put the call on speaker.

'A deal? Well, as I have no use for those two useless bastards now, what say you off them for me and I pay you. Would ten grand suffice?'

It wasn't the deal Harry had expected. Not by a long shot.

'What, you want to pay me ten grand to kill two of your own employees? After you just sent them on a little jolly to kill me? And even though you know that I know exactly what you're involved with?'

'When you put it like that it does sound rather harsh, doesn't it? But you have skills. I can see that. I'm happy to pay for them. And that monstrous face of yours would certainly add a little something to the work I could send your way. As for your little threat about knowing what I'm involved with, really, you have nothing, unless you have me. Which you don't, do you?'

Harry hung up then leaned in close to the man he had held up against the back door of the van. 'Did you hear that, pal? He wants me to kill you! How's that make you feel? Small? Insignificant? Expendable?'

Harry left that in the air for a moment before speaking again. 'Anything you fancy telling me about your supposed employer? You know, like where I can find him, that kind of thing?'

Harry felt the man try to nod.

'Right, then,' Harry said, easing off just enough to let the man speak. 'Tell me everything you know.'

.   .   .

JUST OVER AN HOUR LATER, Harry climbed out of the van and locked it. The two men inside weren't exactly comfortable, of that he was pretty sure, seeing as he'd done his best to make the ride as vomit-inducing as possible, but that wasn't something to be worrying about right now. Not when he had a king to catch.

Harry was now parked up in a picturesque village just south of Bristol. The houses were the kind owned by the rich, despite having at some time been built for the poor.

Harry walked down the road and came to a stop outside the one that corresponded to the address the two men had happily provided him after hearing that their boss wasn't exactly a fan of them staying alive. He rested his hand on the bonnet of the car parked outside—a black Aston Martin—to discover that it was still warm. Then he casually walked up a small path and to a front door and gave it a polite knock. Almost too late, he noticed the tiny glass disc set into it at just below the height of his eyes, and it shattered barely a split-second after he jumped out of the way.

Bastard ...

Harry aimed his boot squarely at where the lock on the other side was bound to be. A second kick was all it took, and the wood crashed inwards to thwack into a wall. Harry wasn't exactly itching to race inside, now that he knew the person he was after was armed, but he didn't have much choice. Not now.

Edging through the door, Harry gripped hard the only weapon he had to hand: a brick from inside the van.

A noise up ahead had him freeze, then a shot rang out and, diving for cover, Harry threw the brick down the hallway and in the general direction of where it had come from. It flew hard and fast into a glass vase, smashing it to pieces.

Harry heard pained swearing. Then he was up onto his feet and racing towards it. At the end of the hall, he swung left to find the man with the suit holding his right hand in agony, covered as it was in slivers of glass, and bleeding like a bastard.

Harry saw the gun on the floor and kicked it out of the way.

'Right,' he said. 'Now, where were we? Ah yes, I remember now. That photograph . . .'

CHAPTER FOUR

'Yorkshire?' The word rolled around Harry's mouth like a sour gobstopper, only he couldn't spit it out. 'But that . . . it's up north!'

It was the Monday after all the fun and games of the previous Saturday and Harry was sitting in an office which could, he'd frequently observed, easily win awards for being anally organised. Even the rubbish in the bin looked neat, like it had been folded first before being chucked away. It wasn't a big office by any stretch of the imagination, but this was the police and anything bigger than a few metres square was a conference room. And the police didn't have conference rooms. If you wanted lots of people to meet together at the same time, you just had to use what was available. Which was usually a quick gathering around the broken coffee machine. Booking a room for a meeting just wasn't a thing.

The only other person in the room with Harry was Detective Superintendent Alice Firbank. He'd worked with numerous detective superintendents in his time on the force, but never one quite so bloody-mindedly professional.

Most people had something you could hold over them, no matter how small. Could be anything, from always using someone else's milk in the fridge and never buying their own, to getting inside tips from someone at the bookies. But Firbank? She was as clean as the proverbial whistle, so clean in fact that Harry suspected she'd buried the damned thing up her undoubtedly spotless arse to make sure no one else could use it. Her black hair was always pulled back in a neat bun, like she'd stapled it there years ago and then varnished it in place for good measure. Her face was a thing of calm wonder, and no matter how irate she sounded, or how sweary she became, the placidness never left. And when she stood up, her average height and trim frame seemed to be magnified simply by the fact that she was speaking, her voice the only thing which didn't quite fit with the rest, because it had a gravelly, snarly edge to it, the rattle of a high-performance engine, or a machine gun on full auto.

'Well, at least your geography is on point,' the DSup said. 'I was rather wondering if I'd need to show it to you on a map.'

Harry really couldn't believe what he was hearing. Okay, so the job hadn't exactly gone to plan, but they'd bagged the bad guys, right? So, shouldn't they have been grabbing a beer instead of doing whatever this was? Yes, she'd explained it all in a phone call the day before, but hearing it now, face to face, it seemed almost too much to believe. And with so little time to prepare as well, he was reeling more than a little.

'You can't send me to Yorkshire,' Harry complained. 'You just can't. Because, you know, *Yorkshire* . . .'

'It's not prison,' sighed Firbank, as though she was discussing something with a particularly grumpy teenager.

'I'm not putting you away. You won't be doing time, well, not as such.'

She grinned then, and Harry had the truly horrible feeling he wasn't so much a colleague, as prey.

'It's a secondment. Think of it like an exchange programme if you want. We're sending you there in exchange for, well, for you not being here, if I'm honest.'

Harry leant back in his chair and stared at the ceiling. If it was at all possible, even that looked neat and tidy. Did the DSup actually clean up there as well? It was spotless. 'But Yorkshire though,' Harry said, his eyes searching for a speck of dust, a cobweb, anything up there which would show that the DSup wasn't actually perfect. 'I've been there. I know what it's like. It's wet and, well, you know, *northern.*'

Harry knew he wasn't doing well here. And it wasn't that he had anything against the north or Yorkshire as such, just that his only memories of it were really only linked to going on exercise when he was in the Paras. And that had generally meant a forced march or *TAB or T.A.B.* through muck and mire, eating cold ration packs and sleeping in wet doss bags. It had been fun, in a masochistic kind of way, but it had meant that his impression of anything up north was more than a little bit tainted. And back then he was young and stupid. Now, he was old and wise. Well, he was old. Ish.

'It will be a chance for you to expand your horizons,' the DSup offered. 'Think about your career, what you want to do with it.'

Harry's head sagged back down and he stared across the desk, the vast, clean desk, with not a thing out of place on it to be seen, just a pen, a pencil and a Filofax—yes, a sodding Filofax—lined up as though they'd been placed there with the aid of a set square and a ruler.

'My horizons don't need expanding, Ma'am,' he said. 'I've seen the world, remember? I joined the army to do exactly that! This is home. It's where I belong now.'

'Then a change will do you good.'

'Horseshit,' Harry said, then added, 'Ma'am.'

Harry knew he wasn't getting anywhere, but he wasn't about to give up. 'Look, if this is about the photograph . . .'

'It's about more than the photograph, Harry,' Firbank said, sitting back in her chair, which was not a good sign at all. 'And I don't mean just the state those rat shit arseholes were in when you brought them back! It's about what that damned thing represents!'

'I didn't have much choice,' Harry said. 'They abducted me and were going to kill me. What did you expect me to do?'

The DSup breathed slowly. 'Well, firstly, I didn't expect you to get into such a situation in the first place,' she said. 'And secondly, I expect you to have some control, Harry!'

'I did what was necessary to bring them in.'

'No,' the DSup said, 'what you did was end up in a bad situation because of your own stupidity, then respond in the only way you seem to know how: violently!'

Harry opened his mouth to speak. Then, seeing the look on the boss's face, shut it again. She clearly wasn't in the mood to listen to anything he had to say. Her mind wasn't just made up, it was locked shut.

'They weren't just bleeding and bruised, they were covered in vomit! The stink of it all! And all thanks to you, Harry, and that damned photo!'

'He's never been caught,' Harry said at last, his voice quieter now. 'It's still an open case. I can't just leave it, you know that.'

Firbank raised her left eyebrow barely enough to be noticeable, yet just enough to let Harry know that she really couldn't believe what she was hearing. 'Open? It's been nearly twenty bloody years, Harry! Twenty! You need to let it go, or your career, what's left of it, will be as dead as the proverbial dodo!'

Harry tried to sit back even further in his chair. 'I can't just let it go, though, can I?' he said, his voice quiet, thoughtful. 'What he did, that man . . . Would anyone? Would you?'

Harry stopped speaking because right then his focus turned to not showing the emotion building like a tornado inside him. Memories rushed at him and it was all he could do to stay in his chair and not just stand up and tear the room to pieces. That his own father could do what he'd done made Harry sick to his stomach.

Firbank stood up and came round to sit on the edge of her desk directly in front of Harry. She folded her arms and looked down at him.

'Look, Harry . . .' Her voice was calm, quiet, and dare Harry say it, caring. 'You left home over two decades ago to get away from him. What he went on to do, you're not responsible for it. You can't hold that against yourself forever. It'll destroy you. In fact, it *is* destroying you. And we both know it.'

Harry had nothing to say. The DSup was right, he knew that better than anyone. But it wasn't going to make any difference.

'He's still out there, though, Ma'am,' Harry muttered. 'That murderous shit . . .'

'I know he is,' Firbank replied. 'But thinking you'll ever find him, and ruining your own life trying to, is never going to bring your mum back or take away what he did to you, and especially your brother, is it?'

Harry had so much he wanted to say, so much he needed to get out, but as always, the words just jammed right up inside his throat and refused to come out. He'd tried counselling and therapy, but it was all bullshit, because none of it got even close to dealing with the only thing which would bring an end to it: finding the bastard and putting him away.

The DSup moved back around to her side of the desk and sat down again.

'It's not for forever, Harry,' she explained, leaning forward, her elbows on the desk, hands clasped together. Neatly. 'This is just a chance for you to get away for a while, to do a bit of re-evaluation, that kind of thing. I think you need it. And if you're honest with yourself, I think you do, too.'

Harry hadn't liked this from the off, but with words like 're-evaluation' thrown around, he was liking it even less, if that was at all possible. Next, she'd be suggesting mindfulness training, whatever the hairy bollocks of hell that actually was. He had a feeling that it probably involved drinking herbal tea.

'And I've to go now, is that it?'

'It's Monday now,' Firbank said, 'and they're expecting you tomorrow, as I explained in our phone call yesterday. That should give you enough time to pack and also to pop in to see your brother. Accommodation is arranged. I'm sure you're good to go as it is, right? You've always been the kind of person to have a grab bag ready at the door.' She smiled at that point, trying to make light of it all, then added, with the faintest suggestion of being serious, 'Try to see this as an opportunity, yes?'

The haste of it all had Harry thinking and he asked, 'How long has this been in the pipeline, if you don't mind my asking?' Then he added a, 'Ma'am' just in case.

'It was either this or a sabbatical,' the DSup said. 'At least with this, I thought you might be of some use and also kept a little bit in control. And you may actually enjoy it.'

'But tomorrow?'

'If I'd told you about it early on, you'd have come up with an excuse not to do it. You'd have wriggled, we both know it. This way, I'm sending you, and there's not much—actually there's *nothing*—you can do about it.'

'But surely they already have a DCI,' Harry said.

'They did, but he's, well, he's disappeared.'

Harry didn't like the sound of that at all. 'And what does that mean?'

The DSup gave the tiniest of shrugs. 'Not for you to worry about. You're still Major Investigations, just on the periphery for a while, understand? Now get yourself gone, would you? And while you're away, do us both a favour and get laid. Sex would do you good.'

'One-night stands aren't my thing.'

'That's not what I was implying, Harry, and you know it.'

Harry stood then, knowing there was no arguing. As to the sex thing, she probably had a point. But relationships were complicated. And they got in the way.

'Where exactly is it that I'm going again?'

'Wensleydale,' Firbank said, then added with a pointed finger as though the next point was really important, 'where they make the cheese.'

'Brilliant,' Harry muttered, his soft, gravelly voice rumbling in his throat as he pushed through the door to leave, 'I bloody hate cheese.'

CHAPTER FIVE

THAT AFTERNOON, HARRY WAS SITTING IN A ROOM WITH all the charm and warmth of an IKEA display, if you removed all of the furniture and replaced it with tables and chairs from 1974. Then set it on fire and redecorated it really badly. But this was the visiting room at Bristol Prison, so he wasn't expecting much in the first place. He'd been in plenty of other prison visiting rooms and they were all pretty much the same, with little more than rows of tables and chairs for people to sit at and do their best to have a normal conversation.

While he waited for his brother to arrive, Harry had a nosy around at the others who were waiting. The room wasn't full and those who were there were fidgeting or nervously looking around as though half-expecting to be taken away as prisoners themselves. But that was, in many ways, the point, Harry thought, even though no one would ever really admit it. Prison was punishment for your friends and relatives, as much as yourself. You visit a prison, you have to go through security procedures and restrictions and follow the rules, just like a prisoner. There was even a term for it: secondary prisonisation.

Harry wasn't one for sympathy, but looking at some of them in the room with him, he wondered if there was ever going to be a better way to do any of this. He doubted it. Society needed protecting from people who broke the rules. And those rule-breakers needed putting away. It was that simple. Rehabilitation was a lovely, cosy word, but it didn't work that well, with thirty per cent of prisoners reoffending. Harry had met plenty of serial offenders, people who didn't know any other way to live, who even committed a crime just to get back into prison, because it meant food and a bed. And a ready supply of drugs.

A door creaked open and Harry glanced up to see prison officers walking in with their charges. When his brother appeared, Harry did his best to not show the shock he felt at how the lad looked. Though he wasn't a lad now, was he? He was ten years his junior and that put him at thirty, at least Harry was pretty sure that was how old his brother was. Never had been good with birthdays. It was just the whole kid-brother thing had never really left, and he still blamed himself for what had happened, for leaving him at all, for every messed up bit of it.

Harry stood up and reached out to shake his brother's hand. 'Hey, Ben,' he said, and nodded to the table, which had a few items on it that he'd bought from the café. 'Thought you'd like a drink and a snack. Crunchie bar, your favourite, right?'

The man standing in front of Harry was a shadow of everything he could have ever been. And Harry could see that his brother had lost weight since his last visit, though how that was at all possible he hadn't the faintest idea, seeing as his brother was thin as a rake as it was.

Ben offered a weak smile but didn't shake Harry's hand. When he sat down, he did so awkwardly, as though the chair itself was causing him pain.

'So,' Harry began, doing his best to sound upbeat, 'what have you been up to? How's the studying going? Have you been to the gym? What's the food been like? Is there anything you need that I can get sent in?'

Ben was staring into the middle distance and Harry didn't know if he was listening or not, so he just kept going, as always.

'You'll be up before the parole board soon, right? You'll be fine, I'm sure. And when you're out on parole, we can really sort you out this time, okay? I'll do everything I can to help, you know that, right? Do you want that Crunchie? That's hot chocolate by the way. Probably tastes like piss, but it's all they've got.'

And still nothing from Ben. Just silence, and the staring.

Harry sat back and stared at his younger brother. He'd never been the same, had he? Not since . . . not since it had all happened. And years ago it may well have been, which is what everyone kept telling him, but Harry knew, not least because he felt it too, that for Ben, it was so raw in his mind that it may as well have been yesterday.

'I'm still looking, you know,' Harry said, his voice quieter now. 'He's out there. I'll find him. I promised, right? And I won't stop. I won't. I can't. That's why I joined up. You know, left the Paras to do this, be in the police.'

At last, Ben turned to look up at Harry, the man who wasn't just his big brother in age, but in size. 'I miss Mum.'

Harry nodded. 'I know, Ben. We both do.'

Twenty years . . . Twenty!

'Why did Dad kill her?'

It was the same stuff every time and Harry gritted his teeth as he did his best to stay calm and just answer. 'Because he was an evil man, Ben. That's just all there was to it. Evil.'

'He was my dad.'

'Yes, I know, Ben, but . . .'

'Dads don't do things like that, do they? They don't kill mums. They don't do what he did to me. We must've done something wrong, you know, for him to do what he did.'

Harry breathed deep and slow, keeping himself calm because raging now would do nothing. Ben was Ben and what had happened to him and what he'd seen, the violence he'd suffered, well that had shut him down from that day onwards, hadn't it? No kid should ever have to go through that. Ever. The abuse, the violence, all of it. He was damaged beyond anything Harry could imagine. It was no wonder he lost himself to drugs, just to escape the horrors festering in his mind. And Harry still hadn't been able to bring in the man responsible, which ate at him like battery acid.

'You did nothing wrong,' Harry said. 'I should have been there to protect you.' Harry broke off from everything else he was going to say because he'd said it all before. About how sorry he was, that he should never have left home, that he should have visited more and seen what was going on and done something and dragged that man out on his arse and pulverised his head against a wall before he'd even had a chance to think about what he was going to do to their mum, to Ben.

'Look,' Harry explained, 'I'm going to be heading away for a while, okay? So, I might not be able to visit as regularly, not for the next couple of months or so. But I'll try and sort something out, okay? Try and pop down to see you.'

Ben didn't respond, just peeled back the wrapper on the Crunchie and took a small bite. 'Why didn't you kill him when you had the chance?'

The question broadsided Harry and a chill raced through him, freezing him to the bone. Then, he leaned his elbows on the table between him and Ben and spoke. 'We can't talk about this, Ben. Not here. Not like this. You know that.'

'You let him get away.'

'No, I didn't, that's not what happened, Ben . . .'

'Yes, you did. You let him get away and you let mum get murdered and you let him beat me because you weren't there!'

'NO!' Harry's voice broke from him with such force and volume that everyone in the room turned and stared. A prison officer approached but Harry raised a hand, nodded an apology, and she halted. But Ben was speaking again, only this time the words were laced with tears.

'He said we were his, Harry! That we belonged to him, and that if I ever told anyone about what he did then he would kill us! And I never told anyone! I never did! I never told you, and he still killed mum!'

The prison officer was approaching again and this time there was no way she was going to stop, another joining her to come and deal with Ben.

'I'm going to leave now, Ben,' Harry said, standing up. 'And you need to calm down.'

The prison officers were there now, getting Ben back under control, calmly taking him away from the table.

Harry kept his eyes on his brother as they led him away.

'I need to get a few things ready, that's all. And Ben? You look after yourself now, okay?'

Ben looked back at Harry and the anger in his face had been replaced by a smile. 'Thanks for the Crunchie.'

CHAPTER SIX

FOR HARRY, IT WASN'T SO MUCH ABOUT THE destination as it was about whether or not his vehicle would actually survive the journey and get him there. He'd had a quick look the evening before at Google Maps and found that the trip from Bristol to Wensleydale, to a little place he'd never heard of called Hawes—and that sounded dodgy right away, didn't it?—would take approximately four and a half hours. Harry added two hours onto that immediately. Then made it three. Not just for toilet and food breaks, but because he wasn't entirely sure that his car would be happy going anything above fifty-five.

Harry had never been all that bothered about cars. Just wasn't his thing. He remembered when he was in the Paras how loads of the lads had spent most of their money on flashy wheels, racing around in Imprezas and whatever else they could find that was loud, fast, and after a few tweaks, even louder. Harry, though, had instead rocked up in a small van just big enough for him to sleep in if he ever needed to, and to hold all his kit. Now though, and having lived in Bristol city for enough years to rarely get lost, all he had was an old green Ford Fiesta with enough bumps and scratches to ensure that, should he ever have to sell it, it would be to a scrap dealer. Harry didn't need anything else for getting around the city, and most times ended up either walking or using public transport. And city cars generally got damaged, either by accident or by some drunk idiot deciding to smash wing mirrors off for fun. So, taking the Fiesta north was, he thought, going to be a challenge. Which was why he'd checked the oil and water before setting off almost as though he was taking part in some kind of driver's Holy Communion.

The first part of the journey, leaving Bristol city on the M32 and driving out past the massive blue IKEA before joining the M4, went by with Harry on autopilot. It was a road he knew particularly well and had even enjoyed a few interesting high-speed chases on it.

As the M4 joined the M5 at Almondsbury, Harry found himself wondering if that kind of excitement was going to be a thing of the past, at least for the next while. He had done a little bit of quick research on Hawes and Wensleydale and from what he could gather it wasn't exactly a festering cesspit of crime. Harry wasn't exactly wishing that it was, but he was almost more scared of it being the opposite. The mere idea of being bored and having nothing to do, well that terrified him. He kept busy for a reason because if he wasn't busy then he was alone to think, to remember, and that was a very dark path to tread.

After a little reading on his destination it seemed to Harry that the closest he'd be getting to a high-speed chase would be sprinting through a field to catch a runaway bull, because he was heading to Herriot country, or at least as near as damn it, and that seemed to be about as exciting as things got in the Dales.

The 1980s television series, *All Creatures Great And Small*, which was based on the books by the Yorkshire vet, James Herriot, had been filmed around Wensleydale, and over in nearby Swaledale, and Harry had done his best to watch an episode he'd found on YouTube. It hadn't exactly filled him with joy. A quick web search on Hawes itself had informed him that the only other real excitement to be found in the area was the visitor centre at the dairy where the famous cheese was made. Famous cheese? How was that even a thing? How could any cheese be famous at all? And seeing as he really didn't like cheese, that was already off the list. Harry had even tried to watch an episode of *Last of the Summer Wine*, but the canned laughter had made him want to throw his television out the window.

Harry pulled his attention away from the dull horror he was sure awaited him and, although only an hour into his journey, was already wondering not only if he could reasonably take a break and grab some more food in addition to what he already had with him, but just how far the car would go before overheating. The smell from the engine was one that told him it was already running hot, so lots of stops were going to be required. He'd also managed to sort out a few things to listen to. With the car too old to take an MP3, a pile of battered CDs was sitting in a small cardboard box on the passenger seat, surrounded by various packets of crisps, chocolate bars, and cans of Red Bull, all necessary supplies for the road ahead. He pulled out the soundtrack to *The Blues Brothers* and slipped the CD into the player, hoping it wasn't too scratched.

The M5 was very forgettable, and Harry was almost

thankful when it started to rain, because that at least blocked out the lack of anything worth looking at beyond his windscreen. Then there was the novelty of driving through miles and miles of roadworks, courtesy of the government trying to improve the roads by digging them up and making them worse. It was only when he found that he'd merged onto the M6 at Birmingham and was heading past Lancaster that the scenery started to get Harry's attention. So much so, in fact, that he missed his turn off to Ingleton, probably in no small thanks to the four cans of Red Bull he'd drunk by that point, which had left him feeling pretty much wired to the moon. Rather than turn around, Harry had continued onwards to turn off at Sedbergh, the weather now clear, the hills of Cumbria and the Lake District to his left and the Howgills now before him, which rose from the ground like the humps of some great slumbering mythological creature.

Off the motorway, the roads which greeted Harry were very much like the lanes he was used to driving on in Somerset on the rare occasions he actually left the city. They were twisting things, bordered by ancient walls and farm gates, and Harry found it hard not to push his little Fiesta a bit and race around the hairpins and bends. In the end, it wasn't just sense that prevailed, but the view.

In Somerset, he was used to low rolling hills and numerous villages, most of which had been gentrified to such a degree that they seemed almost too perfect. The closer proximity of larger towns and cities meant that money moved in with the people, property prices went up, and the roads became highways populated by expensive 4x4s and sportscars. Here though, Harry could see that things were a little different. He was immediately struck by the bleakness of the place, the great hills staring down onto thin roads sewn across moorland. Ancient drystone walls were laid across the fells like the thin threads of a giant web cast out by some massive, hidden arachnid. Houses looked lived in and cared for rather than preserved and modernised to be sold on at a massive profit. The vehicles were older and if they were 4x4s then they actually looked like they were used for their intended purpose rather than just to pick up the kids from prep school, or to drive to Babington House for a gin and tonic.

After Sedbergh, Harry found that the road ahead lost its walls for a while as he drove across open moorland. Swathes of green and brown countryside stretched off into the distance, broken only by low clouds rolling across it like phantoms. And the air! Harry couldn't remember the last time he had genuinely noticed that the air smelled, tasted even, of anything other than exhaust fumes or hot tarmac. But here, it seemed to be rich and sweet and alive.

Then, the rain started up again and Harry remembered why being out in the country had, after his time in the Paras, become a thing he wasn't exactly a fan of. And it wasn't just normal rain either, it was a downpour, and the stuff didn't so much fall from the sky, as hammer down out of it and into the ground below with the ferocity of rounds spat out of an automatic rifle on full-auto. The rapid percussion of the drops slamming into the roof of his car was so loud that it drowned out his not exactly expensive sound system. And even with his windscreen wipers on full, he could still barely see where he was going. So, he slowed down and leaned forward so he could make out what was in front of the car bonnet, muttering and swearing under his breath, not least because the vehicle had now started to leak, which it had never done in all the years he'd owned it. Unfortunately, slowing down made no difference at all except to Harry's growing frustration, so he hit the accelerator hard in the hope of getting the journey over and done with as quickly as possible.

The absolute last thing Harry had expected on his journey was to see blue lights in his mirror. He slowed down to let the police car past only to have it flash and thus inform him that no, it didn't need to get past, he just needed to pull over. Immediately.

Harry glanced ahead for somewhere to pull in, did so, then switched off his engine. Was he really being pulled over? And for what exactly? He hadn't been going that fast, had he?

There was a knock at his window and Harry looked up to stare into the eyes of a man about his own age, in a hi-vis jacket, and seemingly oblivious to the downpour he was standing in, the rain pouring down him like he was standing under a waterfall.

Harry lowered the window.

'How do,' the man said, but then on seeing Harry's face stopped mid-sentence and blurted out, 'Bloody hell, mate, what the hell happened to you?'

Harry wasn't quite sure how to reply. How do? How do you do what? What kind of greeting was that? As for the rest, well he was used to it, though admittedly not from a fellow police officer. 'Hello,' Harry said, his voice formal. 'Is there a problem, officer?'

In Harry's mind, the only problem he could see was that the rain outside was now very much coming inside and he was getting soaked as well.

The policeman wiped his face in a pointless attempt to dry it off as well as collect himself before speaking again. Though he didn't stop staring. At all.

'Nowt to worry about, just that your tail light's out, like,' he said at last, the accent as northern as anything Harry had ever heard, half-suspecting that it was something the officer practised at night as part of some government directive. 'Where are you headin'? Oh, and I'm Sergeant Dinsdale, by the way. Matt. Actually, that's Detective Sergeant, isn't it? Completed one of those training courses last month. I'm like the Rebus of Wensleydale, me! Ha!'

'I'm heading to Hawes,' Harry said, ignoring as best as he could the way DS Dinsdale was laughing at whatever joke he thought he'd just made. And what was with the use of *Like*? Like what?

'On your holidays, are you?'

Harry shook his head. 'Not exactly, no.'

'Staying long?'

Too bloody long, Harry thought. And what was this, an interrogation? 'A while, yes.'

'Well, you'll be needing to get that light fixed,' the DS offered. 'Mike'll sort you out.' He then stood back and sort of just stared at Harry's car before ducking back down to the window and asking, 'You've got his number, right?'

Harry said nothing and instead just stared, wondering just who this Mike was.

'Well, you should have, you know? Helps to be prepared. Just a mo', I'll fetch it for you.' The officer jogged back to his car and returned a minute or so later. He handed Harry a card on which the words 'Mike the Mechanic' and a telephone number were printed.

'He's not *the* Mike the mechanic,' said the DS. 'You know, from the band? Mike and the Mechanics? He's a Genesis fan though. Loves them, he does. Early stuff mainly. None of that Phil Collins solo bollocks.'

Harry tapped his hands on his steering wheel, unable to disguise his impatience.

'Right then, you'll be on your way,' the DS said. 'Just get that tail light sorted. Safe journey, now.'

Harry thanked the officer for whatever the hell it was that he'd actually done other than soak him to the skin, wound up his window, turned the ignition key, and eased back out onto the road. Rolling forwards, and making sure to not go too fast just in case DS Dinsdale was still watching, Harry wondered if what had just happened was a sign of things to come: pulling people over in the rain to tell them they had a light out. He was already missing Bristol, and that wasn't a good sign at all.

By the time Harry was closing in on Hawes, the small town only a mile or so away now and the rain having eased off, he was pretty sure that Firbank's ears weren't so much burning as fully and completely on fire. Or at least he hoped they were, because she had sent him here, hadn't she? And for what reason? Because she thought he needed a bit of a break? Because he wouldn't just let it go about what his father had done? Well, Harry thought, if she thought this would break him or change him, she was very, very wrong. He'd put up with it, do as he was told, then get back to where he belonged. And the sooner the better.

Around the next corner, Harry found his way to be blocked by more sheep than he'd ever seen in his life. And then his car died.

'Bollocks,' muttered Harry, and pulled out his phone to call Mike.

CHAPTER SEVEN

Mike was nothing like Harry had expected. But then Matt hadn't been either. Perhaps basing his expectations on a 1980s television show hadn't been the best of plans, but it was all Harry had to go on. That and the world's biggest advert for Wensleydale cheese, the *Wallace and Gromit* movies, oh, and *Last of the Summer Wine*.

Mike had turned up in a clean boiler suit driving a smart rescue van, hitched Harry up to the back, then dropped him in the centre of town, though Harry thought that perhaps that was too grand a term for what was now before him. Mike had then promised to give him a ring the next day with a diagnosis and cost. There were no 'Ee by gums' or trousers held up with twine. He was simply a bloke doing a professional job. And Harry, with no reason to not believe him, had waved goodbye to his car, actually quite amazed it had managed to get as far as it had without any hiccups, and stared out at the place that was to be his new home for the next few weeks. Which reminded him; he wasn't exactly sure how long this apparent secondment was supposed to last, so that was something to check with the DSup when he gave her a call later that week.

Now that he was here, Harry took a moment to take it all in. With the rain gone and the sky breaking up into a patchwork of grey and blue, the world before him glistened and shone. Hawes, for all that Harry could see, was actually a busy town, and not just because it was stuffed full with holidaymakers, most of whom looked retired, Harry noticed. But then it wasn't the school holidays, so that was to be expected. A car park just over the road was full, and another beyond it. And the marketplace in which he was now stood was all abuzz with people carrying shopping, jumping over puddles, dodging Land Rovers and other 4x4s and one or two particularly massive tractors. At one point, a tractor trundled past towing a huge trailer, which judging by the sounds coming from it and the noses stuck out through the slatting, was stuffed full with sheep. Harry could even smell them as they rolled past, the pungent oily lanolin of their fleeces made all the more ripe by the recent rain.

Across the road from Harry was a market hall, the large double doors open to a constant stream of people going in and out. According to the sign out front, it was the weekly market. Harry wondered about popping in, but a quick look at his watch showed him that the afternoon was drawing on and what he needed first was to find out where he was actually working. Not that this was really going to be work, he thought, looking around him. What crime could there possibly be? The place was filled with pensioners on their holidays and farmers; this was not the stomping ground of drug dealers and thieves by any stretch.

Harry checked the details the DSup had given him then pulled up a map of where he was on his phone. Following the directions, he walked through the town to another part of the marketplace to find himself heading down a lane between The Bull's Head Hotel and a shop called The Bay Tree. The Bull's Head looked particularly inviting and Harry was sorely tempted to pop in for a pint but managed to stay focused on the job in hand. Perhaps he'd have a pint later.

The community centre was sat at the far end of a courtyard. To the left was a tearoom and a pet shop, to the right a double garage. Harry wasn't quite sure what he'd been expecting, but a library and customer service centre were probably so far removed from anything he could have guessed that he just sighed, shrugged, and walked in through the door, which was situated at the left-hand corner of the building. At least it was considerably more picturesque than the building in Bristol, which was a block of red brick designed by someone who definitely put function over form.

Inside, Harry found himself in a sort of general reception or public area, with a dozen or so computers on desks to his right, and a building society area in front of him, which was little more than a reception desk and a small glazed office. Just beyond that he could see the library. Harry couldn't remember the last time he'd been to one to borrow a book. Perhaps, he thought, if work was going to be as sleepy as he fully expected it to be, then maybe he'd give it a go. He'd read books before, so he was sure he could do it again.

The main hub of the facility Harry could see was to his left, with a community office help desk and a couple of post office counters. Between the computers and this area, a corridor headed off to what Harry assumed were more offices.

'Now then, you're looking lost. Can I help?'

The only other person in the building with Harry was a

man built like a bull. He was shorter than Harry, but considerably broader. He was also rather dapperly dressed in a waistcoat, smart shirt with the cuffs flipped up to show a rather fancy lining, jeans, and shoes that had definitely cost a few. Harry, being unaccustomed to having complete strangers not only happily start talking to him, but ask him if he needed help, just sort of stood there, not saying a word.

The man reached out his right hand. 'Dave Calvert,' he said. 'Just popping in to post a few things. I work offshore so when I'm home I do all the chores, mainly because it's just me, so there's no bugger else to do them!'

'Oh, right,' Harry said. 'Do you? Well, that's good.'

'So, can I help?' Dave asked. 'What are you looking for?'

'The police station,' Harry said. 'And I think this is it?'

Dave raised an eyebrow. 'Really? Something up? What's happened?'

Harry noticed in the way the man spoke that he didn't just sound interested, but almost as though he was already thinking of ways in which he could help.

'No, nothing,' Harry said quickly, hoping to dispel any suggestion that a crime had been committed and he was here to report it. Although that would make this all considerably more exciting. 'I'm just due to meet up with–' He glanced at his phone and an email the DSup had sent about who he'd be working with. '–James Metcalf or Liz Coates. They're the PCSOs, here, I think.'

'Jim and Liz?' Dave said, looking off into the distance for a moment, as though contemplating something very important. Then he rubbed his chin. 'Jim'll be up at the mart, no doubt. Liz is probably out and about, like. She keeps busy does Liz. Doesn't live in Hawes either, so she's probably back away home now anyway, in Middleham.'

'Mart?' Harry asked, with no idea what the hell it could possibly be.

'Aye, the auction mart,' Dave explained. 'Top of town. Heading out towards Bainbridge. It's on your right. You can't miss it. You the new bobby?'

'Pardon?' Harry was sure he couldn't have heard right. New bobby? He was anything but! Also, how was it this stranger knew about him? At what point was a policeman on secondment news worth spreading? Just how sleepy was it here?

'Heard mention of you coming,' Dave said. 'News travels fast around here. You'll get used to it.'

'I'm not news,' Harry said, shaking his head.

'A new face is always news,' said Dave, grinning warmly.

Harry checked his watch, if only to move on from a conversation that was making him feel a little awkward. He was sure one of the PCSOs was due to be here to meet him and then show him where he was staying. Not the best of starts, really.

'Jim'll be easy to find,' Dave said. 'He'll be the only one dressed like a copper!'

Harry forced a smile. 'No, it's alright. He's due to meet me here, so I think I'm probably best to just wait.'

'Wait for Jim? That's all you'll be doing,' Dave said. 'His owd man's a farmer, so he's probably up there helping him with whatever he's up to. Probably spending money he's not got on some prize-winning tup he doesn't need or summut.'

Harry was liking this less and less. Not only had he been stopped on the way up from Bristol, but his car had broken down, no one was there to meet him at the police station or office or whatever the hell it was, and now he was hearing that one of those who were supposed to be meeting him was off doing something else that had nothing to do with being in the police!

'Look,' Harry said at last, 'can I just make sure that this is the police station? I mean, it says it's a library and a post office.'

'It's not the police station, no,' Dave said, confirming what Harry had been thinking. 'That closed twenty years ago. Community runs this place now and the police are a part of it. Library, post office, even the petrol station up the other end of town, just beyond the primary school.'

'So, you think I'm best to go find Jim, then? At this auction mart place?'

'Yep, get yourself to the mart. You've got a car, right? Parking should be alright now as folk'll be leaving.'

'Yes and no,' Harry said. 'Broke down on the way here.'

Dave nodded like he knew. 'Green Fiesta? Wondered where Mike had picked that up from.'

Harry was already beginning to get the feeling that in Hawes, everyone knew everything about everything. That was as good as it was bad, he knew well enough. Close communities were good at looking after each other. And that often meant they could keep secrets. Though what secrets around here were to be kept he hadn't the faintest idea, except perhaps the recipe for that famous cheese that he wasn't about to try.

'I'd best get going then,' Harry said and made to move, but Dave held him back with a raised hand.

'No need. I'll take you. It's about a mile I reckon, give or take. That suit?'

'If it's not a problem.'

'No bother at all,' Dave said. 'I'm driving out that way anyway, so I'll drop you off.'

And with that, Harry found himself in the passenger seat of a huge pick-up truck, being driven through Hawes. The journey didn't take long, but it gave him a little look at the town. It was certainly pretty, that much was for sure, with lovely stone buildings and a real sense from the number of people milling around that it was a place with a heartbeat.

'You like pork pies?' Dave asked suddenly.

'Er, yes,' Harry said. 'Who doesn't?'

'Well, the butchers is round the other side,' Dave said, nodding out of his window as though Harry had any idea where he was gesturing towards. 'I'm just saying because they're the best in the dale by a country mile and the pies are to die for. Usually take a few away with me just to remind me of home, though they don't last long.' Dave tapped his not inconsiderable stomach proudly. 'Just follow the road round, over the beck, and up the cobbles past the Methodist church. Can't miss it.'

A moment or two later, Harry spotted a low-slung building on their left with a sign outside saying 'Ropemaker at work'.

'What's that then?' Harry asked.

'What it says,' Dave replied. 'Ropemakers. They make ropes. Clue's in the title. Been there for years. As a kid, that roof used to have the best icicles on it! You could snap them off and pretend they were light sabres! Didn't last long, but it was fun, like.'

A place that makes actual ropes? Harry thought. Really? How was that even a thing? What on earth kind of place had the DSup sent him to?

A minute or two later, Dave pulled his truck up outside a large detached house. 'This is the old manse,' he said. 'You'll meet the minister at some point I'm sure. And just up there on the right? That's the mart. My regards to Jim when you see him.'

Harry exited the truck and watched it pull away before crossing the road and heading towards where Dave had directed. Articulated trucks were queuing up to leave the mart and Harry walked up alongside them, the reek of the animals they carried rich in the air. Through some large gates, he found himself in a world completely alien to him, with great sheds filled with animals to his right, the vehicle park off to his left.

The auction mart was abuzz with action, with people milling around and animals being loaded or moved from pens. It wasn't just sheep either, but cattle and even a few goats. Harry realised that a pair of Wellington boots would have probably made a lot of sense, as the ground was a rich tapestry of manure. So that was something to put on the shopping list. He did his best to avoid the bigger puddles and lumps, but in the end, just accepted that his shoes weren't going to be in the best of states once this visit was over. The smell of the place was rich and acrid and crept into Harry's nose like it was setting up camp.

How he was going to find Jim in a place like this, Harry hadn't the faintest idea, but if, like Dave said, the PCSO was here helping his dad, then perhaps the best place to start was the sheds with all the animal pens. So that's where Harry ventured. Once inside, the sound of the animals grew exponentially, caught as it was now beneath the huge metal roof above him. It sounded as though the animals were all calling to each other, complaining about the accommodation, or moaning about the food.

Harry walked down some of the stalls. He'd never been anywhere like it before in his life. And he could see that from the looks he was getting as he strolled along that everyone else could see just how true that was. And it wasn't just that he wasn't wearing Wellies. He was also one of the few not wearing a flat cap. If someone had told him that such head-gear was still worn by anyone other than a hipster, Harry would have laughed in their face. But in Wensleydale, it seemed at least, the cap was still going strong, worn at every possible jaunty angle imaginable.

A tap on Harry's arm caught his attention and he stopped and turned to find himself face to face with a lad in his twenties wearing a stab vest, green Wellies, and a flat cap. 'You must be Harry!' he said and held out his hand.

'Jim?'

Jim nodded enthusiastically. 'I'll be with you in a mo,' he said. 'Just got to shift that great bastard of a tup in that pen over there first. Dad just bought him. You mind giving us a hand?'

Harry had said yes before he'd even realised what he was saying.

CHAPTER EIGHT

HARRY SNIFFED HIS HANDS AGAIN. YEP, THEY STANK TO high heaven. And all thanks to PCSO Jim Metcalfe, his dad, and a sheep Harry was fairly sure had been the size of a Shire horse.

'You'll get used to it, the smell, like,' Jim said, as Harry walked with him down from the auction mart and back into Hawes itself. 'It doesn't so much come off as blend in if you know what I mean. Nowt like it!' Jim then hooked his hands around his nose and mouth and sucked in a deep breath.

Harry couldn't believe what he was seeing. Who would do that? And why?

'Used to be a sweet shop just there,' Jim said, as they walked past some houses and towards a humpback bridge, dropping his hands back down and stuffing them into his pockets. 'Tiny it was. Proper small, like. You couldn't get a cat in there with you, never mind swing it!'

Walking through town with Jim was proving to be entertaining as much as it was educational. He'd grown up in the town and from what Harry could tell, had caused no end of trouble, from stink bombs thrown into an art gallery, to lobbing eggs and removing garden gates on something called *Mischief Night*. Which, to Harry, sounded a little like *The Purge*, just with less death and more children.

'I visit the mart every week,' Jim explained, as they walked over the bridge, which hooked itself over a river that was running fairly dry. 'You know, in case you're wondering why I was there.'

'I wasn't,' Harry answered, though he had been, he admitted to himself, because he wasn't quite sure how helping your family buy stock could be classed as police work.

'It's all about presence, right?' Jim explained as they walked on from the bridge and onto a cobbled road. 'People see the uniform, they feel safe. And anyone out there thinking of doing something dodgy, well, they think twice, don't they?'

Harry smiled inside. He really wished it were that simple. 'What kind of dodgy?' he asked, as they passed the Methodist church on their left and then up to Cockett's butchers on the right.

'Sheep rustling, mainly,' Jim said, and Harry let out a short burst of laughter which he knew immediately from the look on Jim's face he should have worked harder at keeping in.

'Sorry,' Harry said. 'I'm just used to, well, you know, I've never heard anyone say that before. It's a thing? Seriously? Sheep rustling?' He did his best to turn his smirk into something close to concern.

Jim leaned in. 'Gangs come up and nick dozens,' he said. 'It's becoming more and more common. Some of the sods even butcher them on-site, though we've not had to deal with that yet, thank God. Can you imagine what that must be like? Horrific.'

'Gangs of sheep rustlers?' Harry asked. 'You mean there's money in it?'

'Black market meat sells for thousands. That's why I visit the mart. Keeping my eye out for something, anything, that looks strange or off. The bastards need to be caught because one theft can destroy a farm. And they use the mart to check folk out, see what looks like easy pickings.'

Harry noticed that cheerful Jim had faded away to something else. There was a lot more here than Harry had seen at first, that was for sure.

Harry glanced over at the butchers close by. 'That reminds me; Dave says hi.'

'Dave?' Jim said, looking puzzled for a moment. 'Which one?'

Harry thought for a moment. 'Big chap,' he said. 'Built like a wall.'

'Oh, that Dave!' Jim said, the penny clearly dropping. 'So, he was telling you about Cockett's pies, was he?'

Harry gave a nod. 'He was at the community place or whatever it is. Gave me a lift to the auction mart as he said that's where you would be.'

'And he was right! Clever is our Dave.'

'Our Dave? You mean that you're related?'

Jim laughed. 'What? No! Get away with you, man! That's just what we say.' Then he stopped and turned a quizzical eye on Harry. 'So where exactly is it you're from then?'

'Somerset,' Harry said.

'You're a southerner?' There was a hint of either shock,

or fear, or both in Jim's voice and Harry wasn't quite sure what to make of it.

'I'm from down south, yes,' Harry said. 'Born in Bristol. Moved away, but moved back eventually.'

'Not been myself,' Jim said. 'Down south, that is. I've heard it's pretty busy, like. Is it true that no one talks to each other?'

Harry had nothing so instead asked, 'So where am I staying then?'

'Right opposite,' Jim said, and pointed over the road from the butchers.

Harry found himself staring at a corner building with the word HERRIOT's in gold lettering on the side of it. After what he'd seen of *All Creatures Great and Small,* he wasn't so sure he wanted to go in, fully expecting it to be dated and undoubtedly themed on the television series.

'One of the best hotels in town,' Jim said. 'Food's superb. All the meat is from Dave's here, so go with a steak when you get the chance. Then tell Dave how much you liked it and he'll probably give you a free pie or something.'

Harry was sure then that all of this was either an out of body experience or a dream, and that he'd been in some terrible accident and was now lying in some hospital bed in a coma. It had to be the only explanation for everything that was happening because it was all so different, so alien to his normal life that he half wondered if he should punch himself in the face to wake himself up.

Harry checked the time. It was gone six. He'd been up since six just to get here, and the day hadn't exactly gone according to plan. And now he could feel the tiredness creeping in at the corners of his eyes.

'So, what are the bars like?' Harry asked.

Jim laughed. 'Can tell you're from down south. Bars? We don't have bars, we have pubs. You know what those are, right?'

Harry resisted the urge to slap Jim hard across the face for being such an idiot. 'Pubs? Yes, we have pubs as well, Jim. The south of the country isn't outer space! I do know what they are. And regardless of what's been reported, we even drink beer.'

At this, Jim seemed genuinely surprised, like he'd just learned something truly amazing, and his eyes grew wide. 'What? Theakstons and Black Sheep?'

'There are other beers,' Harry said. 'Though I'm more of a cider man myself.'

Jim pulled a face that looked like he was about to throw up. 'Bad experience on that stuff years ago. Put me off forever.'

'That's because you didn't have the good stuff,' Harry said. 'You need a pint of Wilkins. Amazing.'

'No, it isn't,' Jim said. 'Because I drank eight pints of it when I was seventeen.'

'Ah.'

For a moment, neither man said anything. Then Jim sparked up, clearly remembering something important. 'Tomorrow night. You free?'

'I'll need to check my diary,' Harry said, 'but I'm sure I'll be able to move a few things around. Why?'

'Oh, that's great,' Jim said, absolutely missing Harry's sarcasm. 'You like pies?'

'Yes?' Harry said, not so sure how best to answer, because at what point was the answer to that question ever going to be no?

'Excellent! We're having a pie and pea supper at the Board Inn. Meeting at eight.'

'Who is?'

'We are!' Jim exclaimed. 'You, me, the rest of the team! Detective Superintendent Swift is even making the journey over from Northallerton. Or Harrogate. Or both. And that's miles away! He's not the most interesting of blokes, but you never know, he might buy everyone a pint!'

'And we eat pies and peas?' Harry asked, trying to get his head around the idea. 'And that's all?' Harry didn't think it sounded exciting or tasty enough to warrant Jim's enthusiasm.

'Best pies around,' Jim said, clearly salivating at the thought. 'Pastry is to die for. You can have it with mash or chips or both if you want. I always go for both.'

'Of course, you do, Jim, of course, you do.'

There was something about Jim that Harry couldn't stop himself from liking. The lad had the kind of enthusiasm for everything he talked about that a Labrador has for eating. He had no doubt it was irritating as hell after a while, but right now, it was almost infectious, and it served to take Harry's mind off where he was and why he'd been sent here in the first place. And what he'd said about visiting the auction mart, well that made sense. He was out on patrol, gathering intelligence. Good police work that, Harry thought. Showed initiative.

'So, see you tomorrow, then?' Jim asked. 'I'll be at the office for nine-ish if that suits.'

Harry made to leave, but then turned back to Jim and asked, 'Just out of interest, I'm assuming you all know why I'm here, yes? Why I've been sent up from Somerset?'

'You're the new bobby!' Jim said then slapped Harry on

his shoulder like they'd been friends for years. 'It's going to be great to have a new face around the place.'

'Look, we need to get this straight,' Harry said. 'I'm not a bobby. I'm a DCI; Detective Chief Inspector Grimm.'

'Grimm?' Jim asked, then, 'You mean that's actually your real name? I thought Swift was taking the piss!'

'Why would he?' Harry asked.

Jim went to say something but then clearly thought better of it. 'Well, anyway,' he said, 'we'll certainly keep you busy, I'm sure. A lot goes on around here, you know. Wensleydale isn't as sleepy as you may think.'

Harry couldn't help himself and smiled, raising an eyebrow. This drew a look from Jim that Harry would have put money on him not being able to even attempt. There was a shadow behind it, not much of one to be fair, but just enough to show him that regardless of how he presented himself, there was a serious side to Jim. There had been a hint of it earlier when the lad had mentioned the sheep rustling. But it was steelier now and Harry knew he would have to keep an eye on Jim, if only to see what he was going to do next.

'Anyway,' Jim said, snapping the moment of tension like a twig. 'I'll be off, and you'll be heading over there, okay? And if you go for a wander later, take yourself up over the fields to Gayle. Lovely little walk that. And you won't get lost.'

And with that, Jim, the cheeriest PCSO, indeed *person*, that Harry had ever met, headed off up into the marketplace, leaving Harry with his bag and the prospect of many nights ahead in a hotel bed far away from home.

'You found him, then?'

Harry recognised the voice and turned to see Dave

staring at him, arms folded across his chest, standing outside the butchers. He was carrying a white paper bag. Probably had pies in it, thought Harry.

'Yes, thanks,' Harry said. 'Seems like a nice lad. Is he always that cheerful?'

'Aye, mostly,' Dave said, then he walked over the cobbled road to stand with Harry. 'His older brother was killed on the farm years back. Horrible it was. He's basically carried his parents through since then.'

Harry didn't know what to say. 'I'm sorry, that must have been terrible for him.'

'It wasn't great, no. He's a good lad, right enough, like you said. But there's an edge to him as well, if you know what I mean. Fair enough, too, all things considered. He's tough. Thinks he can take on the world given the chance. Probably would, too.'

For a moment, neither man spoke.

'Right, I'll leave you to your evening,' Dave said. 'Try the White Hart if you're after a cosy pint. Friendly, too. That's my local. Maybe see you there?'

And with that, Dave turned away, leaving Harry to make his way up to Herriot's and to get his room.

Later that evening, having ignored the urge to go to the pub and instead filled an hour or so with a gentle stroll around Hawes, Harry was back in his room staring at the ceiling. It was hard to believe, he thought, that just a few days ago, he'd been involved in bringing in some serious criminals. It wasn't much in the grand scheme of things, but he knew that at least with them off the street, a few more people would be safe, wouldn't get hurt. Whereas now? Where was he, exactly? What the hell kind of use was he going to be, stuck out in the arse end of nowhere?

Harry climbed into bed. His last thoughts before falling asleep were of his brother and that no matter what the DSup did, and regardless of the fact that she'd sent him away to try and forget about it all and move on, he would still be hunting down the man who'd destroyed his family. Even if it took him to his last, dying breath.

CHAPTER NINE

Wednesday burst into Harry's life on the edge of sunbeams lancing their way into his room through the cracks in the curtains. He'd slept well, better than he had for as long as he could remember, thanks to the fact that he hadn't had to go to sleep to the sound of Bristol staying up too late and people throwing up on the pavements outside his flat. No traffic either. It had been eerily silent and yet, despite it being a little unnerving, his body had accepted it like an old friend, wrapped itself up in the quiet, and nodded off.

The breakfast which had met him downstairs was nothing short of epic. He'd wolfed down the lot, fried bread and black pudding and all, drained two huge mugs of tea, then headed off into the day full of anticipation and just a little bit of dread. It wasn't the kind of dread Harry would associate with impending doom, more the kind of dread which twists your gut in the moments before you're due to make a presentation to the rest of your team. He was nervous, and it was a feeling he wasn't exactly used to, not unless someone was threatening to shoot or stab him or throw him off a building, all of which he could chalk down to life in the police force as well as the Paras. The quiet life had very much passed him by. Until now.

Outside, the day was bright and cool, though warmth was coming in on the faint fronds of a breeze, and Hawes itself was quiet, certainly compared with the day before. But that had been market day, so Harry figured it was to be expected. He was in many ways amazed that a place as remote as this could ever be that busy, but then again, as it was probably the only place with a few shops for miles, it wasn't as if people had much choice.

After another walk around the marketplace, and seeing nothing new, Harry headed over to the community office. It was edging close to nine, so he hoped Jim would be there soon to open it up and get him settled in. Though he wondered what kind of settling in there would be. Judging by what he'd seen so far, there wouldn't be much of a need for any in-depth induction programme. Hawes was a small place and the police presence clearly smaller still. So what exactly would he be doing other than driving around a lot, doing school talks (which he actually didn't mind doing, if only because it was fun to scare the kids with his face), and counting down the days till he could go home?

Harry turned at the sound of an approaching engine to find the front grill of a black 4x4? Rover? staring back at him like he was food. The vehicle was slung low, the windows were tinted, and everything about it said that the closest it ever got to off-roading was pulling into a petrol station every ten miles to refuel. The driver's door was pushed open and Harry quietly observed the driver step out into the day from the no doubt leather and wood-clad interior that had housed him. Harry watched him as he approached, intrigued. There was something about him that didn't quite sit right, something off. He was wearing a flat cap, but it looked rather too new and was worn pointing directly forward, rather than at a jaunty angle, like everyone Harry had seen at the auction mart the day before. His Barbour jacket was far too shiny and considering the weather wearing it at all seemed like overkill to Harry. The jacket, like the hat, looked new, and was matched by the Hunter Wellies, which were absolutely spotless.

The man approached Harry and, with hand outstretched, sent a grin across his face so quick it was as though he'd been electrocuted. Everything was for show, Harry thought, even that smile, the eyes above it not so much joining in as using it as a disguise. The man was shorter than Harry but was clearly already trying to make up for it by puffing out his chest. 'Hello! Richard Adams. You must be the new constable!'

Harry took Richard's offered hand and shook it and felt the expected squeeze, the show of domination. It didn't get far, Harry's strong and considerably larger hand rendering this initial pissing contest over before it had even begun. He didn't squeeze back, just made damned sure the attempted squeeze attack wasn't going any further.

'New yes, constable no,' Harry said, releasing the man's hand. 'If you're here for Jim he'll be around in a few minutes I'm sure. He's due to be here nine-ish I think.'

'Excellent!' Richard said, as though what Harry had vocalised was the best thing he had ever heard in his life. 'And how do you find Hawes? Isn't it wonderful here? So beautiful! And the hills? It's like a little piece of heaven!' He made a theatrical display of sucking in a deep breath. 'It's why we moved here. To get away from it all. Have a little bit of the country life for ourselves.'

Generally, Harry found that he liked most people. Well, those who weren't trying to screw society over in one illegal way or another. And that was because, generally, most people were actually alright. That didn't mean he wanted to be friends with them all, just that they were okay, and he was happy to talk to them should the need arise and most times they were happy to help. Every now and again, though, like right now, for example, he would meet someone he just didn't like. It would usually take a while to put his finger on as to why he didn't like them, but there were rare examples where his dislike was immediate. And Harry disliked Richard. Immensely. The word 'wanker' sprang to mind as a first attempt at describing him. Quickly followed by 'tool'.

'So, you're not local, then?' Harry asked, as Richard stood in front of him, chest out like some puffed-up peacock, in all his very clearly new or rarely used country attire. Harry couldn't work out who he was trying to impress other than himself. Hawes, Harry had already realised, was populated by people who were what they were, and who weren't going to be taken in by some shiny new shoes, or in Richard Adams' case, Wellington boots.

'Sadly no,' Richard replied, 'but I do my best to try and get involved in as much as I can locally. Parish council, Rotary Club, that kind of thing. Got to be involved, wouldn't you agree?'

Yeah, Harry thought. I see you, Richard, I see you. Because he'd met many others just like him and had found every single one of them to be self-serving, jumped-up arses. It was clear that 'wanker' was going to be only the first of numerous adjectives to describe Richard.

'If you want, I'll let Jim know you're looking for him,' Harry suggested, if only in the hope that the man would leave and that he wouldn't have to try and think of other things to say to him.

'Would you? That would be fantastic, thank you!' Richard replied, turning back to his Range Rover. 'Got a long journey ahead of me as it is! It may be beautiful here, but if you want to get anywhere at all you have to drive for hours! Worth it though, I think, don't you? I tell you, I spend more hours in this truck than I do here, but that's the price of success, right?'

My God this man was a dick, Harry mused, and asked, 'Is there a message for Jim? Anything you were looking to speak to him about in particular?'

Richard paused halfway into his vehicle. 'He'll know what it's about, I'm sure. And I have every confidence that you being here will ensure the matter is dealt with appropriately. See you, tomorrow, then!'

Tomorrow? Harry thought. He hadn't agreed to that at all.

And with that, Richard jumped up into his vehicle, shut the door, then reversed out onto the marketplace, turned around, and was gone.

Harry heard footsteps.

'Sorry about that,' Jim said, walking over towards Harry from a side-alley. 'Couldn't be doing with talking to him right now if I'm honest. Talks a right load of old bollocks. What was he on about?'

Judging by what Jim was saying, Harry was happy to know that his first impressions hadn't been wrong. 'Just said you'd know what it was about. What does he do, anyway? He's obviously not local. And he's about as country as Soho.'

'What gave it away?' Jim laughed. 'No, he's not. Though he's one of those folk who says he has Yorkshire blood in him, like he's here to claim a throne or something.'

'The throne of Yorkshire? There's such a thing?'

Jim's eyes widened. 'I'm taking the piss, mate,' he said laughing, warmth in his eyes. 'But if there was one, he'd be after it, I'm sure. He's a businessman, though he prefers the term *entrepreneur*. Which is a wanky enough term for him, I think. Not sure what the business is in, but it makes him a lot of money because he's managed to get planning permission to build a huge house on the edge of town. And no one's impressed. Not least because of the woodland there, too.'

Harry sensed they were getting to the reason for Richard's visit.

'Some local kids have joined forces with a group of environmental types,' Jim said. 'Can't move for tie-dyed clothes and dreadlocks. They've set up a camp on the land and in the trees to try and stop him. He wants them forcibly removed. We all feel the same about him, though, so we're kind of just ignoring it for the moment. Anyway, shall we get you inside? Time for a brew, I reckon, don't you?'

HARRY FOLLOWED Jim into the building and the rest of the morning was actually busier than he'd expected. Jim was certainly out to impress. He'd even gone so far as to buy a Cockett's Fruit Cake from the butchers, which Harry discovered to his surprise was also a bakery. And it had gone very well with the numerous mugs of tea they'd both consumed. Though Harry had avoided the other food stuff Jim had brought along with him.

'You not having cheese?' Jim asked. 'What's up with you?'

Harry stared at the slab of creamy white in front of him. He could smell it and that was bad enough. It was a crumbly thing, and every time Jim cut a slice, bits of it would fall off like soft snow down a hillside.

'Cheese? With cake?' Harry couldn't disguise his disgusted confusion at the enthusiastically suggested combination.

Jim nodded and popped a bit in his mouth. 'That's how we eat it round here. Don't knock it till you try it. Bloody delicious! Nowt like it, I promise you.'

'I'm sure you do, Jim,' said Harry, taking a bit of a step back from the milky reek. 'But I'll leave it for now, thanks.'

The police presence in the community centre amounted to little more than a room through the door that Harry had seen the day before and was just about big enough for ten people to sit in a circle. It had a few tables and chairs, a desk, a kettle, and a fair number of whiteboards and noticeboards. Harry, while enjoying another slice of the rather excellent cake, had walked over for a look and found himself presented with the truest picture of crime in the dales he could have ever asked for.

Jim had been right about the sheep rustling it seemed, because one whiteboard was given over to this alone, with lots of notes, information on the victims (the farmers as well as the sheep) photographs, and so on. It was clear now why Jim was taking it so seriously. Harry also saw information on farm death statistics, something about animal rights activists causing damage on a local shoot, a very small area given over to the anti-development demonstrators on the site of Mr Richard Adams' proposed new house, and another board given over to ways to help people drive safely.

'Everyone drives like idiots around here,' Jim explained, coming to stand beside Harry.

It was mid-afternoon now and the lunch of pies and cake, again from Cockett's, was making Harry realise that unless he did something soon, the dependency on that one shop could lead to him putting on a few stone very easily.

'They think knowing the road makes them invincible,' Jim continued. 'Don't get me wrong, the roads are great fun to drive on, but everyone knows someone who's lost someone because of them, if you know what I mean.'

Harry absolutely did. 'So, is this it, then?' he asked. 'This is what you're dealing with most days?'

Jim finished off his cake and cheese and shook his head. 'Crime report book is over here somewhere,' he said through crumbs. 'I'll grab it for you in a sec. Probably a bit different to what you're used to though, right?' At this, Jim moved in closer, like he was hoping to share in some massive secret. 'So, were you involved in lots of serious crime busts, like?'

'What about an incident room? Or somewhere to interview people?'

'There's a few other offices here,' Jim explained, nodding vaguely towards the rest of the building. 'We just make do with what we have.' Jim's face broke then into one of excited anticipation. 'So, come on then! Tell me about life as a copper down south! Gangsters and stuff, I bet!'

Harry paused for a moment. It was clear that Jim was hanging there waiting for something really juicy and dark, no doubt based on what he'd gleaned from too many television crime dramas, where everyone ran around a lot, looked serious, got shot at, swore, and did things the police just weren't allowed to do. Ever. But he knew he had to give Jim something, and it felt a little like giving a reward to a very excited puppy. 'It's not like the movies,' he said at last, 'if that's what you were thinking. But I did get shot at over the weekend. I wouldn't recommend it.'

Jim's eyes pretty much popped out of his face. 'Shot at? Seriously?'

'It's not something I'd make up, I assure you.'

'Bloody hell,' Jim said, letting out a long, slow breath. 'You're a proper serious detective, aren't you? So, why is it you're here again? I mean, being a bobby, that's a bit of a step down, isn't it?'

'Secondment,' Harry said, holding in his frustration. 'Not a bobby. I'm here to learn and to share ideas. And I'm stepping in while something's sorted out with your other DCI, though I don't know much about that. Now, what about that crime report book,' he then reminded Jim. 'Would be interesting to have a look through it, if that's possible.'

'Aye, no bother at all,' said Jim, and scurried off across the room. 'Oh, and Liz will be over later. She was due to be here this morning, but she's got caught up. Farm accident. Nowt too serious, thankfully. Some old bugger drove his grey Fergie into a ditch. He's okay, but she's sorting all that out.'

Harry had no idea what a grey Fergie was and decided, for the moment, to keep it that way.

Jim was now at a locked cabinet on the floor and dropped down on his haunches to open it. 'You looking forward to tonight, then? Meeting the team?'

'Yes,' Harry said, without really thinking, because he

wasn't really sure that he was. 'Anything I need to know beforehand?'

Jim shrugged. 'Nah, I think I'll just let you make your own conclusions. Matt should be here later as well, but I don't know what he's up to, like. He's gone a bit mysterious lately.'

'Matt?' Harry said, putting two and two together. 'Matt Dinsdale?'

'You've met him?'

Harry nodded, but didn't go into the details.

'He's the DS,' Jim said. 'Been a sergeant for years, but finally got around to taking one of those detective course things and now he thinks he's Sherlock bloody Holmes!'

'Thus the mysterious thing?'

'That'll be it,' Jim said. 'He'll probably try and pin you down with loads of questions. Doubt he'll get shot at round here, though.'

Harry was about to say something when a knock at the door interrupted them.

Harry noticed Jim look at his watch. 'You expecting someone?'

'The exact opposite,' Jim said. 'It's gone four now and we don't generally get callers this time of day. Not unless it's properly serious, like.'

Harry walked over to the door. Opening it, he came face to face with a woman who looked like her world had just fallen apart. Harry had seen it before all too often and that sixth sense he'd developed during all his years in the police was suddenly burning red hot.

The woman pushed past Harry as though he wasn't there and ran over to Jim.

'Jim! It's Sophie!'

Jim stood up and faced the woman.

'Mrs Hodgson? What's happened? What's up? What's with Sophie?'

'She's gone!' the woman said and burst into floods of tears.

CHAPTER TEN

JIM LED MRS HODGSON TO A CHAIR AND SAT HER DOWN, pulling one over for himself to sit on beside her. Harry noticed this immediately and was impressed. If Jim had wanted to intimidate, then Jim would have had the chair directly in front of her. Instead, he had gone to the side, which was kinder, non-threatening, and usually helped put people at ease. Obviously, such a technique could be used for all kinds of reasons, and Harry had used it himself to get on the right side of the wrong people more times than he cared to remember, but to see it used here and so deftly, impressed him.

'Right then, Mrs Hodgson,' Jim said and glanced over to Harry to get him to come over. 'This is Detective Chief Inspector Harry Grimm. He's from the south.'

Harry noticed that Jim said that last bit as though he was revealing something truly astonishing, almost as though he was telling this Mrs Hodgson that he was from another planet.

'Grimm?' Mrs Hodgson repeated.

'As in the fairy tales,' Harry explained, then pointed at his scarred face and added, 'though it's a pretty good word to describe this, right?' Harry broke into a smile, but Mrs Hodgson was unmoved.

'He's going to be with us for a while I think,' Jim explained. 'Helping us out on a few things, seeing how we work up here, sharing ideas, that kind of thing. So, do you mind if he joins us? Would that be okay? He's a proper detective. Someone even shot at him at the weekend!'

Harry was already beginning to regret telling Jim the little that he had.

Mrs Hodgson looked up at Harry and he saw reflected in the horror in her eyes that the sight of him was more than enough to have her say no to Jim's request. The being shot at information probably hadn't helped much either.

'But, his face,' she said.

'It was an IED,' Harry explained, realising his earlier attempt at humour had failed terribly. 'An improvised explosive device. I was in the army before the force. Trust me, I actually looked worse before this happened.'

The joke, designed to ease the tension, raised a smirk and a knowing, appreciative nod from Jim, but not a thing from Mrs Hodgson.

'Look, if you don't want me here, I can wait outside, it's fine,' Harry offered. After all, he was the new kid on the block and he didn't want to get in the way. Not yet, anyway. He was pretty sure he would at some point.

Mrs Hodgson shook her head. 'No, you should stay. Help Jim find my Sophie. And please, call me Martha.'

Harry walked over and grabbed a chair of his own. He placed it near to Jim's and a little further back so that it was very clear Jim was running things for now.

'Right, tell us about Sophie,' Jim said, pulling out the standard-issue pocket notebook, or PNB, to jot down his notes and observations. 'What's happened exactly? And just take your time, okay? There's no rush.'

As Martha began to speak, Harry made a few discrete observations of his own. Mrs Hodgson, *Martha*, was in her mid-forties, conservatively well dressed, and considering she was reporting a missing daughter, unsurprisingly very distressed. She wore a cross made of two roughly hewn nails around her neck and was clutching her handbag like it was a shield. Though Harry had no children of his own—at least he was pretty sure he didn't—he fully understood what he was seeing because he'd seen it before all too often.

The last time he'd had to deal with something similar, the statistics had shocked him: approximately 100,000 teenagers run away each year in the UK. That figure had seemed so large that he had thought it must be wrong. But it wasn't. From what Harry had seen of the area so far, however, he could think only that this was a kid looking for attention, nothing more. She would probably turn up under a friend's bed by the end of the day. Hardly the most exciting case he'd ever had to deal with, but he still took it seriously, because you just never knew.

Martha was clearly finding it difficult to speak.

'In your own time,' Harry said. 'Just say what you can, and we'll see how we do, okay?'

'Yes,' Martha said. 'Thank you.'

'Here,' Harry said, and passed her a napkin from over by the kettle.

The woman wiped her eyes and then started to speak. 'We had a call from the school this morning,' she explained, sniffing through the words. 'They asked if Sophie was ill because she wasn't there. But she left home and caught the bus this morning like she always does!'

'And you're sure?'

Martha nodded. 'She was gone when I got home this morning.'

Her voice broke on her words, and to Harry, it certainly sounded and looked like her world was falling apart and that she was struggling to hold it together.

Harry asked, 'So you were out?'

'Yes,' Martha said, wiping her nose again and working well to pull herself together. 'I'm a carer. It's what I do, I care. And I have early appointments. So, I'm usually out before Sophie, you see? She catches the bus at seven-thirty. It's quite a trek to Leyburn, but it's the only secondary school so there's not really much choice, is there?'

'And how long does it usually take, the journey I mean?' Harry asked.

Martha paused for a moment. 'I think she usually gets in at around eight-thirty, eight forty-five? Depends on the weather though. It can be terrible in winter. Buses get stuck, break down. Sometimes they get to school only to be sent home again.'

'Why's that?' Harry asked.

'Most of the kids from this end of the dale are farming families,' Jim explained, while Martha tried to gather herself. 'Snow comes in, school has to get them back home so they can help get the sheep in or with anything else that needs doing. Just the way of life up here.'

Harry had no doubt about that. The place seemed to live and breathe farming. 'Why didn't you call?' he asked. 'If you knew this morning she was missing, I mean.'

Martha wiped her nose and eyes. 'Because we didn't

want to make a fuss,' she said. 'For all we knew she was just skiving, like most kids do sometimes. But school's over now and the bus has come back and she wasn't on it!'

'Can you think of anything that could have caused her to run off?' Jim asked.

Martha shook her head and blew her nose. 'Nothing, not really, anyway. You know how it is with teenagers; they get so upset about the smallest thing and make such a big deal about it, and then it all blows over and is forgotten.'

Harry caught this and went with it, hoping Jim wouldn't mind him jumping in so much. As he still wasn't sure what his role was or what he was going to be doing, he thought he may as well just at least pretend like it was any other normal day on the job back down in Bristol. Well, as close as he could, anyway; Martha certainly didn't come across as a thug or drug dealer. The mere thought made Harry smile, and he quickly shut that down before either Jim or Martha noticed.

'So, she was upset about something, then?'

Martha turned to face Harry. He could see that her eyes were bloodshot to hell. She'd obviously been crying for a lot longer before she had arrived. 'Yes, well, I think so, but you know teenagers. Why would she run off? It makes no sense.'

Harry pressed further. 'Do you know what she was upset about? Was it something at school? Something at home?'

'Well, we were at church on Sunday,' Martha explained, 'and Sophie had a bit of an outburst and she was very upset so we had to leave. Some message on her phone. And then she got into trouble at school on Monday, which is unusual really, but again, she's a teenager, so I suppose it's to be expected, isn't it?'

'Who was it from?' Harry asked. 'The message I mean, the one she received on Sunday?'

'Her boyfriend, clearly,' Martha said, wiping her nose. 'Who else would it be? Teenagers and their relationships! Honestly, it's as though it's the end of the world for them, isn't it, if they have an argument or break up?' She sobbed a little more, dabbing at her eyes with a hanky. 'Where could she be? It makes no sense!'

Jim said, 'She's run away before, hasn't she?'

Harry raised his eyes at this.

'That was nothing and it was a long time ago,' Mrs Hodgson said, dismissing it with a wave of her hand, which was clutching the now-soggy napkin. She looked awkward though, Harry thought.

'It's still important,' Harry said, leaning in a little. 'If she's done this before, then there might be a pattern or a trigger or something.'

'Well, she didn't get far,' Mrs Hodgson said, her voice a little sharp. 'She never does. She was hiding at a friend's house and George had her back in hours. This is different! It isn't a pattern!'

Harry sat back again, thinking over what he was hearing, and what he knew from experience. Most teenagers took to running away due to one of three things or, in some cases, a combination of them: bad communication between them and their parents, being unable to deal with a personal problem or mistreatment or abuse either by their parents or another adult. Rarely was it anything else. And Martha certainly wasn't coming across as the kind of person who would do something to harm her own child. Though Harry knew better than to take that as read.

'Who's George?' Harry asked.

'My husband of course,' Martha replied matter-of-factly.

'Did he see her leave this morning?'

Martha shook her head. 'He was in bed with a migraine. He gets them a lot. Awful they are. And they were worse after the weekend with Sophie's behaviour. He's very sickly. Always going down with something or other. Sometimes I think I'm more like a carer than a wife!' She laughed, but a sob buckled the sound. 'But that's what marriage is, isn't it? In sickness and in health?'

'So where is he now?' Harry asked. 'George, I mean.'

'Home,' Martha said. 'In case Sophie comes back. He works from home as a bookkeeper so at least he doesn't have to travel. And he has his podcast thing to prepare for as well. For the church. He's been up and about this afternoon, but that's all. We're both so worried! But I've told him to take it easy and not do anything that will make him ill again. He gets ill so often.'

'A church podcast?' Harry asked, monumentally surprised that the woman sitting in front of him would even know what one was.

'Yes, it goes out live every Wednesday evening. It's for everyone who can't attend a service or doesn't want to come to church officially. You must listen later! It will do you good. I do the Bible readings for it.'

Harry was noncommittal with his nod at Martha's suggestion.

Jim spoke next and Harry noticed that the open page of his PNB was already looking full, not that they'd learned much so far. 'I assume Sophie broke up with her boyfriend late last night, then? And that's why she's run off?'

'I honestly don't know,' Martha said. 'I just know that she's gone. And the trouble she's caused by doing it, as well. Not just to George and I, but to the school, and now you, the police! Honestly, when she gets back, she will have some explaining to do. To everyone!'

'The boyfriend, you've called him, I assume?' Harry asked.

'He's not seen her, or that's what he says,' Martha said and there was a sliver of anger now in her voice. 'He's older, in sixth form. Has a motorbike as well, would you believe? I'm sure she's just doing it to upset us. It's very distressing. It's no wonder George has so many migraines. I'm surprised I don't get them myself.'

'And why would she do that?' Jim asked, getting in just before Harry had the chance. 'You know, go out with someone to upset you?'

'Would you approve?' Martha snapped, her words sent like barbs. 'She's fifteen! It's, well it's wrong, isn't it? We try to stop it, but we can't just lock her away, can we? He's not a bad boy at all, in fact, he's actually a lovely lad, it's just that she has so much else to be getting on with, and there's her exams. Who would be a parent?'

Harry quickly shuffled through everything that they had been told.

'So, she received the text on Sunday, had a bad day at school on Monday, and she's waited till today to run away. Correct?'

Martha gave a short nod.

'And there's nothing else you can think of that would have caused her to do this now?'

'No! Of course not! Why do you keep asking?'

'Because,' Harry said, 'I'm trying to help, and we need to ask questions, even if it's difficult to find the answers. As you said, she has run away before.'

Mrs Hodgson nodded. 'Yes, of course. I'm sorry. I understand. And like I said, that other time was nothing. Nothing at all.'

Harry looked over to Jim, who took the hint.

'This is what we're going to do. We will need to do a full search of your house, even though we know you've already done it. Her room may be able to tell us something. We'll put Sophie on the National Crime Information Centre Missing Persons File. We will call every friend, every neighbour, every person who knows Sophie, who knows you, to see if we can find anything out about how she's been, what's happened, and where she might be. I also want you to call the National Runaway Switchboard and leave a message for your daughter, because she may call in.'

As Jim rattled off everything that was about to happen, Harry could see that this news stilled Mrs Hodgson's nerves a little. He was also once again impressed by Jim. PCSOs weren't always taken that seriously by the public, nor by some in the police. Jim, though, Harry believed, could single-handedly rectify that in a heartbeat.

'Do you have a recent photograph of Sophie on your phone?' he asked. 'I know everyone knows everyone around here, but I think we need to put something together, a poster, and get it out far and wide so that everyone is looking for her. And we might be able to check her phone and track it.'

Martha looked either baffled or confused by this. 'Track her phone? What do you mean?'

'GPS,' Harry said. 'Might be able to find where she is based on that, especially if you have a tracking app on it. A lot of parents do. I know I certainly would.'

Martha pulled out her phone. It was a brick and from the way she was holding it clearly weighed a ton. Harry couldn't remember the last time he'd seen one like it. Didn't everyone have smartphones now?

'I don't really do very well at all with technology,' Martha said, waving the phone a little, drawing Harry's eyes to the evidence supporting her ignorance to the modern world. 'I leave that to George. I can just about manage a text! George can email you one later, but I do have this.'

'So, no tracking app, then.'

'A what's that now?' Martha said looking confused, displaying the phone on her outstretched hand as though this was show and tell at school and Harry was the teacher. She then reached into her handbag and handed a photograph over to Harry. 'That's her,' she said. 'That's Sophie.'

Harry took the photo and did everything he could to make sure his face, no matter how messed up it already looked, was impassive. Deep down, what he wanted to do, what every copper wanted to do, was reach over, and tell Martha that yes, they would find Sophie, and promise them that everything would turn out fine. But that was a rule Harry had never, ever broken, and never would: you never made a promise you couldn't keep.

The girl in the picture was thin and pale. If she was going for the goth look, Harry thought, then she had nailed it. She was sitting at a desk and the photograph showed her in the middle of some school work he assumed.

'See? She's very studious,' Martha said, almost as though she had read Harry's mind.

Harry stood up. 'So, let's go and have a look at her room, shall we?'

CHAPTER ELEVEN

THE HODGSON'S HOUSE WAS A LARGE SEMI-DETACHED ON the road leading out of Hawes on the right, a few hundred metres past the playpark. It was certainly a grand place, standing back from the road behind trees and a large lawn. Harry glanced along the road as they walked up to the house, noticing how many of the other residencies were equally impressive. They were the kind of houses he could only ever really dream of buying, and if they were moved down south the price of them would be astronomical. Though he had no doubt that up here they were already far beyond what most of the local population could afford.

'Nice place,' Harry said, if only to break the quiet which had ghosted over them on the walk down from the community office.

'Yes, it is,' Martha agreed. 'It was left to us by my father. I'm, I mean *we* are very lucky.'

At the front porch, which had a very nice pitched roof with slate tiles, the windows in the walls and door of stained glass. Harry hung back. 'Mind if I just take a scooch around? I'll catch you up.'

Jim gave Harry a nod and then allowed Martha to lead him inside.

Now on his own, Harry took a wide walk around the property. The day had warmed up considerably and even though it was late afternoon, the air was dry and crisp, and Harry took off his jacket. The lawn at the front had little to show other than the fact that it was a very well-tended lawn, the edging absolutely straight like it had been cut with a razor. He walked around it, imagining what it must be like to have a garden like this, one you could sit out in and enjoy, rather than his own rear yard which, Harry admitted, he hadn't exactly done anything with since buying the place a decade ago. But he'd had other things to occupy his time, like work, and well, work. If he was honest, and he was rarely anything else, he was already struggling to regard what he was doing now as work; having a nosy around a nice garden in the kind of place people visit to go on their holidays, looking for evidence to help them find a teenage girl who, he was sure, had run off just because she was a bit upset, and her parents didn't understand. It wasn't that he liked looking for trouble, just that he was good at dealing with it. And this, so far, didn't strike him as trouble, just a lack of communication between parents and child.

Lost in his thoughts, it wasn't until Harry was back around at the front porch that he realised he'd missed something and quickly retraced his steps. There, in the far front corner of the lawn, the edging wasn't as sharp as it was elsewhere, like it had been worn down, though there was no reason for it to be so, unless George had slipped or pushed too hard on his edging tool, Harry thought. He dropped to his knees and looked at the flower border between the edge of the lawn and the wall between it and the pavement beyond. Some of the plants, he noticed, were broken. Only a little, and he only noticed because he was looking, otherwise, he would have missed it. It was probably nothing, Harry thought, and when he spotted a few clumps of animal hair, he figured that's exactly what it was: a big fat nothing in the shape of a cat.

Jogging back up to the garden, Harry made his way around to the side of the house. There wasn't much to see except for a large, well-built garage, the side of the house to his left, and beyond, a garden leading out to fields. A black Nissan Qashqai was parked in the drive, and in front of it a red BMW, which wasn't what Harry had expected at all. Seemed a bit showy for someone like Mrs Hodgson, he thought. Harry had a quick look and saw nothing out of the ordinary about it. The car was maintained well, that much was obvious. He checked the garage and found that it was open. Sliding the up-and-over door, he momentarily imagined finding a sheepish Sophie hiding inside, but sadly that wasn't the case. A little bit too much to ask, perhaps, Harry thought. The garage was neat and tidy, orderly. Everything had a place—a lawnmower and other garden implements hanging on labelled hooks in the wall, a Brompton folding bike, a mountain bike, and a tidy workbench that didn't exactly look like it got much use.

Back outside, Harry saw that the side of the house was almost as impressive as the front, if only for the huge, sturdy metal drainpipes running down it from the roof. There was also a small wooden door, painted black, leading to a cellar perhaps, Harry thought, and that was something he'd always wanted, ever since he was a kid. Back then, it had been the idea of a little den all of his own, a secret hide-away. But as life had gone on, that had turned into the strangely romantic notion of a cellar filled with wine. It wasn't even that he liked wine that much, but the idea of having lots of dusty racks filled with the stuff, well, he could see how that was rather attractive. Perhaps even have an upturned barrel as a table down there, some candles on it to light the place, and a couple of chairs by it to sit down on and share a bottle of red with a friend or two. The problem with that was it required Harry to have friends, and since leaving the Paras he'd been more of an acquaintances kind of man.

Harry moved on round the back of the house to find a garden that was picture postcard perfect and had a to-die-for view over open fields and the fells beyond. It looked almost unused, the kind of garden tended and cared for, to be looked at rather than lived in. It certainly wasn't a garden for barbeques, he mused.

Harry made his way back around to the front of the house and as he did so he found his eyes wandering up the drainpipes. They were, like the rest of the house, cared for, well maintained, the shiny black paintwork glistening in the light of the day. About halfway up the wall, Harry noticed some scuff marks, not on the drainpipes themselves, but on the brickwork they were screwed into. Probably from a ladder, he thought, because he guessed that anyone Martha was married to would be the kind of person to check their drainpipes and guttering on a regular basis. And good for them, too.

Back at the front of the house, Harry made his way inside to find Jim and Mrs Hodgson standing with two other men.

'Harry Grimm, I assume?' said one of the men, walking

over and reaching out with his right hand. 'I'm Steven Hurst, the church pastor.'

Harry shook the man's hand and found himself looking into the face of a middle-aged man with styled hair, an expensive shirt, and designer stubble. He couldn't have tried harder if he'd tried harder, Harry thought. And he guessed that this man was the owner of the red BMW.

'Pleased to meet you,' Harry said, not exactly sure if he was or not. The pastor had the kind of smile he had seen a lot in his life, one which was full of charisma and charm and always hiding something.

'Martha called me,' the pastor explained. 'About Sophie. So, I popped over to offer a little support to her, to the family.'

'Did you? Oh, right,' Harry said.

'And now that you're here I'll be going.'

Harry stepped back as the pastor made his way past him to the front door, before doubling back and first shaking George by the hand, before hugging Martha. George, Harry noticed, didn't seem best pleased with either action, judging by the way he seemed to almost flinch at the man's touch.

'I'm sure Sophie's fine,' he said. 'God's got his eye on her, I'm sure of it.'

Then he was back past Harry and out to his car in the drive.

The other man stepped forwards.

'George, yes?' Harry said, shaking the man's hand as well. 'Harry. Harry Grimm. DCI.'

Harry hadn't exactly been expecting the same approach as he'd experienced with Richard Adams, a handshake used as a power trip, gripping hard, twisting, as if to do so was to be the alpha male. But George was so far and away from this that Harry almost flinched, as the man didn't so much grip his hand as rest his fingers in Harry's palm and wait for him to do something with them. The man's fingers against his skin felt like he'd just opened a pack of cheap sausages, their flesh cold and soft and a bit damp. The man himself looked deathly pale, with sunken eyes and clothes which hung from him like washing on a clothes horse. The clothes struck Harry as a little odd, with the day being so warm, and here was George dressed in a thick, green winter pullover and brown corduroy trousers. He was pulling at the cuffs to the jumper as well, so that they covered not just his wrists but the base of his hands, too. This was a man who really felt the cold, Harry thought. He wanted to put the man's behaviour and general demeanour down to the fact that he was undoubtedly deeply concerned about his daughter, but he sensed there was more to it than that. Martha had mentioned that he was the sickly type and he certainly looked it as well as acted it.

'Pleased to meet you,' George said, his voice so quiet that Harry leaned in so that he could hear it better. 'Well, not pleased, obviously. I mean, oh dear, poor Sophie . . .'

Martha rested a hand on George's arm and he flinched a little at her touch. 'It's fine, darling. I'm sure DCI Grimm knows what you mean. Are you sure you shouldn't still be in bed?'

George looked at Harry and said, 'I get a lot of pain, you see? Headaches and such like.'

Harry smiled and said, 'So, is it okay if we have a look around?'

With swift approval from Sophie's parents, Harry and Jim started to walk around the property while Martha, Harry noticed, led George through to the lounge to sit down.

The ground floor, which contained the lounge at the front, had a grand, high ceiling hall, with stairs leading up to the next floor. At the end of the hall, there was a dining room, a kitchen, and a utility room, which led out on to the back garden. In the kitchen, Harry noticed an empty cat food bowl on the floor.

'Reminds me of my mum and dad's place,' Jim said, knocking a knuckle against the wall under the stairs. It gave a hollow ring, as much due to the wooden panelling it was made of as the space hidden underneath. 'I mean, the house is totally different, seeing as it's a farmhouse and no way near in as good a nick as this place. They have stairs like this, but there's a door to a cellar, which still creeps me out! Dad hangs pheasants down there. It's proper creepy.'

'He what?' Harry was looking at the stairs but was taken aback by what Jim had just said. 'He hangs pheasants? But that's animal cruelty! Who the hell hangs pheasants?' Harry's mind was suddenly full of images of an old man stringing up squawking fat birds by their necks and leaving them to die.

Jim stared at Harry as though he was talking in another language. 'You hang them after they're shot,' he explained. 'Allows the meat to mature, develop a bit of extra flavour.' Jim's face broke into a grin. 'What, you're not? No, you can't have thought that . . . Ha! That's hysterical!' Jim tried to stifle his laugh but it didn't quite work.

Harry, for the briefest of moments, wanted to slap the laugh off his face. How was he supposed to know what he'd meant? The closest Harry ever got to a pheasant was either the squashed ones on the road or the stupid ones that would seemingly forget they could fly and just keep on running down the road in front him. He'd certainly never eaten one. Not that he wouldn't, it was just that pheasant wasn't something he would find down at the local Tesco in the ready meals section. 'Not from round here, remember?'

'But hanging pheasants? You ever tried catching one? Why do you think we shoot them?'

'That's a question to which I have no answer,' Harry said. 'It's not something I've done or really had any interest in.'

And it wasn't. Harry wasn't a vegetarian by any stretch of the imagination, and in the Paras, he'd not killed any animals to survive as such, but he'd skinned a few rabbits (and eaten a few worms) while out on escape and evasion training. The idea of killing something to eat wasn't something he had a problem with, it was simply an activity he'd never been in close proximity to. Living in Bristol, the only wild animals he'd had access to were the pigeons that woke him up every damned morning. Here though, he could understand why it was more the norm. Wherever you looked, the countryside stared back, almost as though it was beckoning you to head out for a walk.

Jim shrugged. 'Well, I'm sure we can sort that out for you while you're up here, like. Won't be pheasant, not the season, but some rabbit or something.'

Harry said nothing and instead walked to the stairs and headed upwards, past the first landing with a doorway standing open leading off to a bathroom, and up to the second, from which led off five further doors.

A five-bedroom house, Harry thought. Some folk really did have it better than the rest.

'Sophie's room is at the front on the left,' came a call from the lounge and Harry glanced back to see Martha staring up at him. 'It's a lovely room. Double aspect. I hope it's not too messy. And I need to leave rather soon, if that's okay. Will you be long?'

'No, shouldn't be,' Harry called down and saw Martha walk away from the stairs and into the lounge.

Harry and Jim popped their heads around the doors of the other rooms on their way, but didn't give much consideration to them, only noticing that they were neat, tidy, perfect. The doors to each room had been stripped back and re-stained, the grain of the wood shining through. Even the period handles and locks had been refurbished.

'Bloody hell,' Jim said, as they moved between the rooms across the somewhat expansive landing. 'They've got some money, right enough.'

In the smallest room was a little desk with a computer and a microphone and a single bed. On the wall were racks of neatly labelled CDs. The others were all double rooms, each with a double bed and expensive furniture.

'I can't really imagine George doing a podcast,' Jim said, staring at the equipment. 'He's not exactly charismatic, is he? But he's been doing it for a while now. Goes out live every Wednesday evening, without fail.'

On entering Sophie's room, the first thing Harry noticed was just how tidy it was. No, it was more than tidy, it looked as though it had been deep cleaned.

The bed was larger than a single, but not a double, Harry noticed first of all, and it wasn't a cheap flat-pack job either. This thing was solid wood, expensive. The rest of the furniture was made to match and included a huge wardrobe, a desk, and a little set of drawers with a mirror on top. A few framed photos were sat on top of the desk and the drawers, but other than that there were no other ornaments. The desk was a workstation, that much was clear, with a desktop computer and neatly arranged files, all labelled with different school subjects. A Bluetooth speaker stood off to the side. Under the desk was a rubbish bin containing what looked like a box of pills, scrunched up and discarded. Harry crouched down to have a closer look. He wondered if he would find the pill, thinking that in a religious household like this one, the discovery of such could certainly cause a serious argument and perhaps, with Sophie, enough to have her run. The box was labelled 'Aconite'.

Harry rose to his feet and realised then that the desk was the one from the photograph Martha had just shown them, the one of Sophie. On the wall, which was the only decoration in the room at all, was a timetable, which Harry noted didn't just cover school time, but evenings and weekends as well. Looking closely, it was clear that Sophie was a studious kid, with little free time left once she had done all her work and the additional tuition and lessons he saw pencilled in. What on earth did she do for fun, he thought? In the corner of a room he saw something plugged into the wall. It looked like an electric cooler, not that the room needed one, despite the heat of the day, it was cool inside.

Harry scratched his head.

'Something bothering you?' Jim asked.

'This is a teenager's room,' Harry said. 'But if it wasn't for the desk and the folders, you wouldn't know that, would you?'

'How do you mean?'

'Where's Sophie's stuff?' Harry asked, walking around the room now, glancing out of the window to the front of the house, then the one at the side, which looked out over the garage, one of the huge, metal drainpipes just visible. 'There's no television, no games machine, and it's just so damned neat and tidy. I know kids don't do posters now, at least I don't think they do, but this place just doesn't feel like it belongs to anyone at all!'

Jim walked over to Harry and leaned in conspiratorially. 'Look, Harry,' he said, his voice quiet. 'Let's just say they're a bit of an odd bunch and leave it at that, eh?'

Harry scrunched up his face, confused. Martha and George seemed to him to be the very definition of harmless. Just two people living a quiet life and trying to deal with a teenage daughter, which was never an easy thing to do. 'How do you mean?'

'Oh, they're harmless,' Jim said. 'And Sophie's lovely, if not a bit sickly herself. Takes after her dad, I think. They're just a bit religious, if you know what I mean. And you've met the pastor now, too. He's always out and about, trying to get more folk to go along to his services. I've heard he even does magic at them! Can you imagine that? A vicar sawing someone in half!'

'Not quite sure I know what you're getting at,' Harry said.

Jim was clearly wrestling with a way to try and explain what he meant. 'They're churchgoers, which is fine, loads of folk around here are, but they don't go local, to the chapel, like. They head down the dale to Leyburn. Out of town. It's one of those modern churches, uses the gym hall at the secondary school. Happy clappy.'

'And what's that got to do with anything?'

'You saw her phone? They're just a bit like that. Nice people, just a bit out of touch and a bit clean.'

It was Harry's turn to laugh. 'A bit clean? That's your reason to regard them as an odd bunch, is it, Jim? You should visit Bristol some time; I could introduce you to a few people who would really make your eyes pop out of your head, trust me.'

And I'm one of them, Harry thought.

There was a cough at the door and Harry turned to see Martha standing there staring at them both. 'I'm going to be heading off now. Is everything okay?'

'Yes, it's fine,' Harry said. 'Can I just ask what that is over there?' He pointed at the device plugged into the wall.

'It's an air purifier,' Martha said. 'Sophie needs it for her breathing.'

'Really?' Harry asked. 'Is she asthmatic?'

'She just needs to be careful,' Martha said. 'That's all.'

Harry shrugged, none the wiser. 'And these?' He showed Martha the pills from the bin.

'For her anxiety,' Martha said.

'Why would she throw them away?' Harry asked.

'I honestly have no idea,' Martha replied.

Harry wasn't so sure that Martha was being entirely truthful. 'We could do with a look through the drawers and wardrobe, but seeing as this is a girl's room, I don't think it's appropriate that myself or PCSO Metcalfe do it.' He could see that Martha was relieved to hear this and turned to Jim to ask, 'This other PCSO, Liz Coates? When was it you said she was getting here?'

'She's on her way, like I said. Texted me while you were out in the garden. Thought she'd get over early to meet you before the supper this evening.'

Harry looked to Martha. 'We'll have PCSO Coates have a look through Sophie's things. If you're happy with that?'

Harry couldn't quite tell what was going on in Martha's mind as she chewed over what he had said. Then she nodded her agreement and headed back into the house, calling back to them that George would be able to answer any further questions, that she'd be leaving soon.

'So, Liz then,' Harry asked. 'How long is she going to be?'

As Jim went to answer, the sound of a motorbike engine revving loudly broke into the moment. 'I think she's here,' he said.

CHAPTER TWELVE

BACK AT THE COMMUNITY OFFICE IN THE MARKETPLACE, having had a call from Mike the mechanic that all was good with his car for him to pick up the following day, the afternoon was now drawing into early evening and Harry was settling down with another mug of tea. He turned down the cake and cheese and watched as Jim and Liz both hoovered up a plate each of the weird combination. Harry just couldn't get his head around it. Yes, the cake was good, excellent actually, so why add cheese to it? How was that even a thing? The idea of it made him gag.

One of the whiteboards on the wall had been cleared to make way for missing Sophie. Her photo was front and centre and that was about it, except for the scant details they'd learned so far, that she'd caught the bus to school, but hadn't actually turned up, none of the contacts had seen or heard from her, and that she had run away once before. Harry had looked at the details about that incident. There was nothing of use from it in the file, just that she'd run off and, as he'd learned earlier, been found at a friend's. So, the likelihood was that the same was true again and that Sophie would soon get bored and turn up the next day.

PCSO Liz Coates had arrived in motorbike leathers, having turned up in the drive of the Hodgson's house on a dirt bike that looked far too big for her to climb onto, never mind ride. Harry may have towered over her in height, but then as she looked barely a touch over five foot, most people probably did. It was pretty obvious though that she wasn't the kind of person to be intimidated by anyone or anything. Not that Harry had been trying to intimidate her in the slightest, only that he was aware that sometimes, his height, coupled with his face, could have that effect when meeting someone new. Her curly brown hair was pulled back in a ponytail and her eyes fairly sparkled, Harry noticed.

At the house, Liz had quickly got on with the task in hand, having first had a quick chat with George and Martha. She knew them, that much was clear, and it only went to re-emphasise what Harry had already suspected about Hawes and the surrounding area: everyone knew everyone else. So how any crimes were actually committed he had no idea, because surely as soon as one was, everyone knew about it.

Having searched through Sophie's bedroom, Liz had come up with nothing that could suggest either where Sophie had run off to, or if there was anything other than the text on Sunday to have caused it. She had found several boxes of medicines and strange little bottles of liquid, which on closer examination had turned out to be nothing more than some homeopathic remedies. Not exactly something Harry was into, but each to their own, he thought. He had half hoped to find at least a badly made spliff tucked into a sock, because that would have given them a little bit more to go on. Regardless, Martha was upset; George, he assumed, was as well, but it was hard to tell, and he was more convinced than ever now, after Liz's search, that Sophie had just gone to hide at a friend's house for a reason as yet undiscovered or undisclosed. He just hoped that it wouldn't be long at all before she would be back in her sterile room, probably working up another reason to bolt.

Something had been bothering Harry about the Hodgson's house and he hadn't been able to put his finger on it at all. It was only later, when they were back at the community office, that it had struck him how, upstairs, all the rooms had been pretty much identical. Even Sophie's. Who lived like that? No individuality at all. Hardly suspicious though. Each to their own and all that. It was just a house that was run like clockwork, he suspected, and the person in charge was very clearly Martha. And if being neat and tidy, and using homeopathic remedies and air purifiers made you happy, then why not?

Tea, cheese, and cake finished, Liz and Jim were back on the phones, running through the list of contacts Martha had given them to call. So far, they'd come up with nothing, but what they were doing was all they could do until either Sophie turned up, she contacted her parents, or someone gave them a tip.

'So, what's life like as a city detective then?' Liz asked, ticking off another name on the list of contacts she was calling about Sophie.

'He got shot at last weekend!' Jim said, still far too excited about the information. 'Can you imagine that?'

Liz actually nodded her head, which surprised Harry. 'I was beating on a shoot as a kid, right? And this idiot, a paying gun with no bloody idea at all, he took a bird so low that the head beater saw the shot go over my head by barely a couple of foot! He just took a crack at a bird before the beat had even started! Wasn't even at his peg! And there he was with this fancy side-by-side with all its engraving and his tweed.'

Harry hadn't the faintest idea what Liz was talking about so just nodded to feign interest.

'So, what happened?' Jim asked.

'His gun was taken off him, head beater gave him a right dressing down, and he was kicked off the shoot and sent home.' Liz then looked up at Harry, who was leaning against the wall. 'Should've shoved his silver hipflask up his arse as well, if you ask me.' She smirked. 'Do you get shot at a lot, then?'

'It's not an essential part of the job, no,' Harry said. 'And I try to avoid it whenever I can.'

'What kind of gun was it?' Jim asked.

'An illegal one,' Harry said. 'Look, like I said, it's not like what you see on the TV, I promise you. I'm not Luther.'

'Pity,' Liz said. 'He's well fit.'

'And I'm not?'

'You've seen your face, right?'

'Fair point.'

'It's the same round here, too,' Liz then said. 'You know, most folk think it really is *Last of the Summer Wine* or *All Creatures Great and Small* up here, that we all *ee by gum* at the drop of a hat. But we're pretty normal really.'

'Aye, lass, 'appen there's nowt wrong wi' us, like,' Jim said with a wink.

Harry wasn't so sure. 'What about the cheese and cake thing though? That's not normal.'

At this, Liz and Jim both laughed.

One thing Harry already liked about them was that they didn't hold back in getting to know him. Most people would skirt around the fact that his face was the kind of thing a special effects producer for a horror movie would be proud of, unsure what to say, whether to say anything at all. But these two weren't just okay with it, they were freely making it a part of the banter. And he hadn't even been here a full day. Was everyone really this friendly?

The door crashed open.

'Alright, there!'

Harry turned to see Matt Dinsdale stride into the room.

'Now then, Rebus!' Jim said.

Matt laughed. 'Aye, that's me! A detective!' He glanced over at Harry. Recognition lit his face. 'Bloody hell! Fancy the new bobby being you! How's the car? Did you get that tail light fixed?'

'I'm not the new bobby,' Harry said, barely disguising the irritation in his voice. 'Why is it that everyone keeps saying that?'

Harry saw a look pass between the three of them. 'Is there something you're not telling me?'

They all shook their heads.

'Probably best to have a chat with the DSup later on,' Matt said. 'Anyway, what's going on?'

'Missing person,' Harry said. 'Sophie Hodgson.'

Matt crashed himself down into a chair. 'She's gone again, has she?'

Harry picked up on this. 'How do you mean? Martha, Mrs Hodgson, said she'd only done this once before.'

'Officially, yes,' Matt said. 'Because that's the only time they reported it, got us involved, like. But she's buggered off a few times has little Soph. Shame really, she's a smashing wee lass, though she doesn't half look like she could get blown away in the breeze.'

Harry brooded for a moment.

'You alright?' The question was from Liz.

'Just wondering why Mrs Hodgson didn't say that earlier when we spoke to her.'

'Probably didn't think it was important,' Liz said. 'Like Matt said, there was only one official time.' She turned her eyes to Matt. 'What were the others then?'

'It's only what I've heard,' Matt explained, 'but I think she's run off a few times, usually after an argument or something. She was no bother at all until she went down dale to Leyburn, to the secondary school. It's a big change, going from the primary school here to having that bus journey twice a day and the big school. Some kids fare better than others. Just think poor Sophie finds it difficult. Still remember when I went. Terrified me. She'll be back soon, I'm sure. Now, who's for a brew?'

Harry declined. So far, he'd drunk more mugs of tea in the past twenty-four hours than he had in a normal week. Did they drink anything else? Not even coffee? Yorkshire, he was sure, was going to take some getting used to.

WITH THE CLOCK edging towards seven-thirty, Harry gathered up the mugs and gave them a wash, figuring they would be heading off pretty soon to whatever this pie and pea supper was that had been promised. He'd expected to meet the rest of the team beforehand but that obviously wasn't the case.

'Harry,' Jim called from the corner of the room. 'Come and listen to this!' Jim was staring at his phone.

'What is it?'

Jim turned his phone around so Harry could see the

screen. 'It's the website for the church the Hodgson's go to,' he said. 'George is doing his podcast! Thought you'd like a listen!'

Before Harry could do anything about it, Jim cranked up the volume. From the tiny speaker on his phone came George's voice.

'And he does this every Wednesday?'

'Yep, never misses a day. Does it live, like I said, apparently because it's more real or inspired that way.'

'And he does a whole service?'

'More than,' Jim said. 'Once this one is done, which goes on for an hour and a half, he then does all kinds of stuff, from an hour or two of songs recorded at church, to Bible readings and additional sermons and whatnot. Usually finishes around midnight.'

As Harry listened, George's voice was replaced by a female one, only this was considerably more dramatic, perhaps a little too much so. Then it dawned on him who it was. 'That can't be!'

'It is!' Jim said. 'Martha does the Bible readings! She's very into drama. Takes it seriously. She's actually rather good. The local drama group performs in the Market Hall a few times a year. You'll have to pop along to their next show!'

Harry's phone rang. He recognised the number. 'I'll just be a minute,' he said, glad of the excuse to not listen to the George and Martha show anymore. He popped out of the room and made his way outside to answer. 'You wouldn't be checking up on me now, would you, Ma'am?'

'That's exactly what I'm doing,' Firbank said from the other end of the line, down in Bristol. 'You made it there, then?'

'Of course, I did,' Harry said annoyed that he was being

made to feel like a kid on a school trip. 'So, is there a reason for this call beyond making sure I've not buggered off on holiday?'

The DSup was quiet for a moment.

'What is it?' Harry asked, never a fan of silence on the other end of a call.

'It's Ben,' the DSup said. 'He's fine, it's just that –'

'Just that what?' Harry said, cutting in. 'What's happened? And why do you know first and not me? I'm his bloody family!'

'And it's me that's informing you instead of the prison, Harry, so wind your neck in!'

Harry took a deep breath. 'Go on.'

'His meeting with the parole board has been cancelled. Random search of his cell found drugs. And you know the rules as well as anyone, Harry. He's in there because of drug offences as it is. He wants to get the parole board to take him seriously, this isn't the way to do it.'

Harry was confused. 'But he's clean now,' he said. 'That's what the reports have said. And he's been a good lad, right? Quiet. This doesn't make sense.'

Harry sensed that the DSup was working out how to say what she wanted to say next.

'It does if he doesn't actually want to get out.'

Harry laughed. 'Well, that's horseshit nonsense, if you don't mind me saying so, Ma'am! Of course, he wants to get out! Why the hell wouldn't he?' Then a thought stabbed hard into Harry's mind. 'Is this about Dad?'

'I don't know for sure,' the DSup said. 'But it's all I can think of.'

'You think he's been in touch with Ben? But that's impossible! Why would he do that?'

'No, that's not what I think,' the DSup said. 'But perhaps Ben just feels safer there, that's all. You know as well as I do just how many offenders actually reoffend so that they can get back into prison. It's a way of life for some of them, and it's safe, or safer than being released. Food, a bed, a roof over your head, company.'

'I need to come back. I need to see him, talk to him, find out what's going on.'

'No, you don't.' The DSup's voice was sharp and forceful. 'You're not away on a jolly. You've replaced a missing DCI, remember? And you don't get to decide. You work for me, remember?'

Harry laughed and the sound was cold and hard. 'This isn't work, Ma'am, and you know it! You know what amounts to crime around here? Sheep rustling, tourists getting in the way, dangerous driving, and a teenager who's decided to do a runner because she broke up with her boyfriend! It's a complete bloody joke! And you're making me look like one sending me here!'

Harry's rage burned in him then. He'd done well up to now with heading north and had even found himself to be enjoying it all, which had come as quite the surprise. But now, with this news, it was clear that he needed to be back in Bristol. Wensleydale was a sleepy place and there was no need for him here. It was a complete and total waste of time. And he wasn't finished, not quite yet.

'As to that missing DCI? That's a wind-up, isn't it? Because everyone seems to think I'm the new sodding bobby! So whatever bollocks reason it is you've come up with to have me sent up here, you need to sort this shit out and get me back down south!'

The line went quiet. Harry was breathing hard, adrenaline burning in his veins. He was in the mood to lash out, smash things, crack skulls.

'I suggest, DCI Grimm,' the DSup said at last, her voice measured and yet filled with menace, 'that you think very, very carefully about how you speak to me the next time we talk. Very carefully indeed.'

The line went dead.

'Everything okay, Harry?' Harry turned to see Jim staring at him. His cheery demeanour had vanished.

'Yes, everything's fine,' Harry said, stuffing his phone back into his pocket.

'Okay then,' Jim said. 'We'll be heading off to the Board Inn in a couple of minutes.'

Harry nodded that he understood and Jim went to head back into the community office, but turned back to stare up at Harry.

'I know this isn't Bristol,' he said, his voice quiet and serious. 'I know it's not what you're used to, with all that exciting crime and whatever the hell else you get to deal with. And I guess you won't get shot at up here.'

Jim paused, took a breath, and Harry could see he was working hard to remain calm. 'But it's where we call home,' Jim continued, 'and we keep it safe. If you think it's a joke, then that's on you.'

And with that Jim pushed the door open and stepped inside, leaving Harry alone with his thoughts.

CHAPTER THIRTEEN

On arriving at the Board Inn, Harry had found the rest of the team to be already waiting for them, that being Detective Superintendent Graham Swift, Detective Inspector Gordanian Haig, and Detective Constable Jenny Blades. The DSup had turned from the bar at which he was standing to meet Harry halfway across the floor, though with the speed it took him to get there, Harry had almost reached the bar by the time they met.

'Harry Grimm, I assume?' the DSup asked, almost as though he wasn't entirely sure. 'Yes, definitely you. I can see that.'

Harry ignored how the DSup was now staring at his face as one would a museum piece. The man was late-fifties and was wearing the kind of pullover and trouser combination worn by someone who favoured brown and beige above all other colours and bought their clothes from free catalogues pushed through the letterbox advertising exceptionally comfortable shoes.

'That's me,' Harry said. 'Pleased to meet you, sir.'

The DSup, though, was laughing quietly, rather than listening. 'Is everything okay, sir?' Harry asked, glancing at Jim as he walked past them and over to the bar.

The man nodded. 'It's just your name, you see,' he said. 'Grimm.' He did air quotes with his fingers. 'And here you are, where you are. It's all rather amusing, isn't it?'

'Is it?'

'Yes, of course, it is! Can't you see it? Your name? And here? Altogether it's rather superb!'

No, Harry couldn't see it. Not in the slightest. And he was now beginning to feel not just a little bit awkward, but annoyed and marginally unwelcome to boot. And after Jim had made him feel, and not without reason he'd realised, he was half tempted to make his excuses and leave. 'I think you'll have to explain it,' Harry suggested.

The DSup turned and led Harry to the bar, raising a finger for one of the bar staff. 'What'll you have, DCI Grimm?'

'It's Harry. And I'll have . . .' Harry glanced at the pumps at the bar and couldn't see a cider in sight. He also noticed that everyone except for Jim and Matt were drinking beer, who were both sipping from bottles of alcohol-free stuff. Which meant they were probably on call for the evening, he realised, the rest taking the opportunity to kick back a bit. 'Theakstons?' he finally said, mainly because it was the only beer he recognised the name of.

The DSup ordered Harry 'A pint of best, please,' and handed it to him when it was brought over.

'Cheers,' Harry said, and took a sip. It was dry and there was a subtle sweetness to it. Not bad, he thought. Not bad at all.

'Anyway, as I was saying,' the DSup said, 'your name and here.'

'Yes, about that,' Harry replied, still baffled.

'You're Grimm and you're here, up north, aren't you?'

'Yes, I am, sir. Can't deny it. The hills and the accent are definitely the biggest clues.'

'Well, that's just it, isn't it? You're Grimm, up north? See? Grimm up north, but with two Ms instead of one! It's what you southerners say about up here, isn't it? That it's grim up north? And here you are! Grimm up north! But I'll call you Harry, if you don't mind. We're a small force up here, you know. First name basis and all that. Try to keep things friendly.'

Harry really had to force his face into a smile. Not quite a smirk, and definitely not a laugh, but a smile. It was the best he could manage, though he had a feeling that what he'd actually managed to do in the end was to make his face look like someone was slowly pushing a knife into his side. And the scarring only made that all the worse. 'Ah, yes, I see that now. Funny, sir. Yes, very clever.'

Swift was still chuckling to himself as he introduced Harry to the other two members of the team. 'Harry, I'd like you to meet Detective Inspector Gordanian Haig, and Detective Constable Jenny Blades. Ladies, this is Harry Grimm, as in grim up north! Isn't that marvellous? Dear me, I do crack myself up sometimes, you know.'

Harry took in the two people now facing him. To his left was Gordanian Haig, owner of a name he'd never heard before in his life and of a face stern and hard, though the laughter lines from the corners of her eyes suggested much of that was a mask. At least he hoped it was. To his right was Jenny Blades. Whereas Gordanian was probably in her early fifties, Jenny was clearly considerably younger, mid-to-late twenties, Harry guessed. She was tanned and slim and had the look about her of someone who spent most of her free time keeping fit.

'Hi,' Harry said. 'Good to meet you.'

'Well, that's a face only a mother could love,' Gordanian stated, her thick, almost tuneful Scottish accent taking Harry rather by surprise. 'I'm assuming you didn't do that on purpose. And just so you know, everyone calls me Gordy.'

'You're Scottish,' Harry said, stating the bleeding obvious.

'Aye, I am that,' Gordy said. 'Can see why you made DCI. And to think I'm not even wearing tartan or walking my haggis in with me. How do you do it?'

Harry laughed, though felt a little awkward. Gordy, he could tell right away, didn't take prisoners. 'IED,' he explained, motioning at his face with a finger. 'I was in the Paras before the police.'

'You're a glutton for punishment then, I see,' Gordy said.

'It doesn't show that much,' offered Jenny. 'I mean, it does, but it doesn't. You carry it off.'

'I'll take that as a compliment.' Harry smiled. 'Thank you.'

'So, how are you settling in?' The question was from Swift who Harry noticed seemed to hover and float around the others, not exactly taking part, but neither was he not involved, or at the very least, listening to what was going on. It was a bit creepy.

'So far so good,' Harry said, thinking that summed it up best, though his mind was still on what his own DSup had told him on the phone. He was also still very aware that Jim had overheard everything he'd said, and he needed to make a good impression. 'It's a beautiful area. You're all really lucky to live and work here.'

'You think so, do you?' Gordy said. 'You don't find it all a bit wee? The hills and whatnot?'

'Shut up, Gordy,' Matt called over. 'Just because Penhill isn't Ben Nevis! If you don't like it, you can always bugger off back across the border, you know.'

'What, and miss all the fun I'm having here? Get away with you, man!'

Jim stepped up beside Jenny. 'It's not got the crime you're used to though, has it, Harry?'

'That's a good thing, Jim,' Harry said making a point of looking directly at him. 'Trust me, you don't want around here what I've had to deal with back in Bristol. You're better off for it.'

'That we are,' the DSup said, butting in. 'Now, who's ready to eat? I believe the tables are all ready.'

Harry shuffled in with everyone else over to where they were all then sat down and was handed a menu.

'So, what's with this pie and pea thing, then?' Harry asked Jenny, who was sitting next to him.

'It's a Yorkshire thing,' Jenny explained. 'Pie and pea suppers have been going on for donkey's years. What are you going to have?'

Harry looked down the menu. 'Steak and ale sounds good.'

'It is,' Jenny agreed. 'Good choice. You going for chips, mash, or both?'

Harry had honestly thought Jim had been joking. 'You mean both is a thing?'

Jenny laughed and the sound was bright and clear. 'Of

course, it is! Get your pie, some peas, a nice dollop of creamy mash, then crispy chips chucked on top. Lush!'

'I'll be going with that then,' Harry said. 'When in Rome, and all that, right?'

It was only when the food arrived that Harry realised just how hungry he really was. He was onto his second pint of Theakston's best and the pie was everything a pie should be. The pastry was crisp and buttery, the gravy rich and delicious, and the meat and vegetables inside not only plentiful but tender. As for the mashed potato topped with chips, now that was a work of genius. Harry couldn't believe he'd never tried it before.

'Good, isn't it?' Jenny said, leaning in close. 'This is the reason I run so much; means I can properly pig out when I want to!'

'Thought you were a bit of a keep-fit fanatic,' said Harry, taking a sip of his pint. 'Must be nice running around here. Used to do a fair amount myself when I was younger. Not so much now though. And by not so much, I mean hardly at all. It's one of those things I try for a couple of months then realise a couple of months later that I've not been doing it, if you know what I mean.'

At this, Jenny's eyes went wide. 'Then you're in the best place in the world to start again!' she said. 'I can take you out on a few easy runs, show you around. You got any kit with you?'

'No, none,' Harry said, relieved actually that this was the truth. He had to do some running every year to pass the police fitness test, but actually doing it as a regular thing? Not for years. And his running shoes were almost satanic, the stench of them close to being classified as a biological weapon.

'Well, Cunningham's will sort you out,' Jenny said. 'It's an outdoor shop in the marketplace. Bound to have something. I'll take you over tomorrow, get you sorted out. How's that sound?'

'Er, well,' was about all Harry could manage. He was full, the beer was delicious and going to his head way sooner than he'd expected it to, and now he was being offered a shopping trip and a fell run. He needed a lie-down. Urgently.

The sound of a glass being tapped rang out and Harry was glad of the interruption because Jenny's exuberance for getting him moving was a little terrifying. He looked up to see Swift standing up.

'Thought I'd better say a few words to welcome the newest member of our team,' he said, his half-full pint glass in his right hand.

Harry felt his gut twist. He wasn't the biggest fan of being the centre of attention.

'Now, as you all know, Harry has been sent up north on secondment to get a feel for the way we do things around here, share ideas, that kind of thing. And also, to help us out after the unfortunate affair with DCI Alderson.'

Harry noticed how, at the mention of the DCI, a few in the team shot sharp looks at each other. So, what exactly had happened to him?

Swift spoke again, cutting off Harry's thoughts. 'I'm very sure we can all learn a lot from Harry and he from us. Let's just hope that trouble doesn't follow him, shall we? We don't want any of that city crime nonsense coming up and knocking on our doors in the dales, now, do we, if that's okay with you, Harry?'

So, things were taking an odd sort of turn, but Harry offered a friendly smile and a nod anyway.

'Excellent,' Swift said. 'And I think we can all agree that the best way for all of this to go well is for Harry to act in the main as a sort of observer if you will.' Swift stared straight at Harry and the relaxed look he had about him earlier was gone now, replaced by steel. 'No getting into scrapes or pushing your nose in where it's not wanted, now!'

The man laughed, but the point was clearly made: he didn't want Harry upsetting the apple cart. Which was a problem, Harry thought, because that was pretty much the only thing he was good at. So, the boss clearly wasn't happy about having him there. Great. Absolutely bloody marvellous.

'Welcome to Wensleydale, Harry!' the DSup called out, the steel in his eyes gone. 'Our very own Grimm Up North!'

The DSup then laughed hard and loud, so proud of his earlier joke that he'd clearly decided to go public with it as part of his little welcome speech. Harry did a very good impression of laughing along with everyone else, then got back to munching down what was left of his pie.

'Don't worry about him,' Jenny said. 'Swift's a funny old bugger. We don't see him that much and that's the way he likes it. As do we. He just wants to get to retirement as easily as possible, I think, and he's probably worried that having some smart city detective up here is going to make that more interesting than he would like.'

With the meal done, Harry thanked everyone and headed off back to his room at Herriot's. It had been an interesting evening for sure and as far as he could tell the team wasn't a bad bunch at all. Gordy seemed a bit on the bizarre side, but that was no bad thing. Jim, he had already got a handle of, though he was a little concerned about what the lad had overheard earlier on. Liz was a firecracker it seemed, busy and wild and honest. Matt was no Rebus, that was for sure, but at least he'd passed as a detective. And Jenny was a bundle of energy. As for Swift, he was definitely someone that Harry decided it would be best to stay away from if at all possible. He had that sort of smiling assassin feel to him and that made Harry uneasy.

Walking down from the Board Inn, Harry was struck then by something he'd almost forgotten existed—stars. Staring up, the sky was black as Marmite and the stars shone back with such rich brilliance it seemed to Harry that he wasn't so much staring up as down, gazing into the deepest, darkest depths of the universe. It made him feel dizzy like he could at any moment just fall up into them.

Finally, back in his room, Harry was in bed in minutes, more aware this time than the night before of the quiet and the dark. And both closed in on him and no sooner had his head hit the pillow, he was asleep.

Harry's phone rang at just gone one in the morning. He didn't recognise the number. Neither was it a time he was ever very happy about seeing because a call at this time was never good news. He stared at the clock on the cupboard at the side of the bed, willing it to explode. It didn't, so he picked up the phone and answered. 'DCI Grimm. Who is this?'

'Harry? It's Jim. It's . . .' Jim's voice broke on the line.

'What is it? What's wrong?'

'A body,' Jim said at last. 'Someone's found a body.'

CHAPTER FOURTEEN

HARRY WAS SITTING IN THE FRONT PASSENGER SEAT OF A police Land Rover which had either seen better days, had a hard life, or both. Probably both, Harry thought, considering the roads and lanes in Wensleydale. He couldn't have sat in the back even if he'd wanted to, full as it was not just with the usual police paraphernalia to deal with a crime scene or traffic, but a couple of hay bales shoved in for good measure.

'I'm dropping them off at the school in the morning,' Jim explained. 'They've got rabbits so we give them free bedding.'

'I thought they'd have sheep,' Harry said, meaning it as a joke, albeit not a particularly good one.

'Not at Hawes they haven't because that's primary. Leyburn, though, they've got their own flock. The school basically has its own little farm. You can do a GCSE and A-Level in all the skills you need to run one yourself.'

'Really?'

Jim nodded. 'Loads of kids do it, most of them from this end of the dale. They know it all anyway, but that little piece of paper is a good thing to have, isn't it? Got it myself, like. Covers the business side of things as well, and you need that more than anything, to be honest. Farming is little more than being in love with what you do and never being out of debt. Just the way it is. It's in your blood.'

'So, it's in yours, then?'

'Sure is,' Jim said.

'So why this? Why a PCSO?'

Jim gave a non-committal shrug. 'Why not?'

Harry could tell he wasn't going to get any more from Jim, but there was obviously more to it than what he was letting on.

For the rest of the journey, the two men sat in the silent darkness, their only company the thrum of the engine and the wind whistling into the cabin from the numerous gaps and holes which seemed to pepper it.

The route Jim took them climbed up the valley side from Hawes. Heading out on the road towards Bainbridge and beyond, and taking a right after about a mile and a half, they had climbed steeply to a village called Burtersett, though from the size of it Harry thought that village was rather a grand term. It had a chapel though, so clearly there was, or had been at some point, enough of a population to support it.

Leading out of Burtersett, Jim had gestured to a large farmhouse on the left on a junction between the lane they were on and another leading away and back down the valley. 'My place,' he said. 'Well, it's not mine, but you know what I mean. I still live there with my mum and dad.'

'Nice,' Harry said, and it was, albeit somewhat bleak, stuck out on its own at the end of the village, a last house on the left almost, though Harry doubted it had ever seen anything like the horrors which had occurred in *that* movie.

The road continued to climb in a straight line for a couple of miles before breaking into a few left and right turns and a bit of dip, before it started to rise again.

'Just going over the old Roman road,' Jim said, not slowing the Land Rover down, so Harry didn't really get a good look. 'Runs straight as you want, from Bainbridge on our left, right up onto Dodd Fell to our right. Nice little walk if you ever fancy it. Kids from the primary school do it each year as a sponsored walk.'

The road then started to flatten off before finally dipping downwards. Then a sharp bend hung them a left and the road grew steeper still. Harry was very aware that Jim wasn't hanging about, and he was reminded then about what the lad had told him the day before about locals knowing the road and driving too fast. So, he braced himself a little more, his knees jammed against the dashboard, his left hand gripping the grab strap above the door.

At a junction with a main road, Jim swung the Land Rover right then left, and Harry noticed that the wheels squealed as he did so, the vehicle leaning a little too much for his liking thanks to the additional suspension and clearance of being a 4x4.

'There it is,' Jim said, nodding ahead. 'Semerwater.'

A minute or so later, they were over a bridge and pulling in onto the shore of the lake, just up and away from another parked car.

'Creeps me out, this place,' Jim said, switching the engine off. The whole vehicle then proceeded to make a new range of noises, clicking and popping as it cooled down and rested itself after the drive over. He then reached into a bag in the passenger footwell and pulled out some plastic slip-on covers for their shoes, handing a pair to Harry, along with a torch. The lad was certainly prepared, Harry thought.

'Why's that?' Harry asked as they both climbed out and he walked round to meet Jim on his side.

Jim shrugged. 'There's just a feel to this place, like. The water's always colder here, like it's darker, more gloomy. Know what I mean?'

Jim had a point, Harry thought. It was a dark and bleak place. The lake itself, Semerwater, stretched out before them, a still thing of silent blackness, like an enormous hole waiting to swallow them. Around them, Harry could make out the watching silhouettes of the surrounding hills. It did seem colder, he thought, as a shiver raced through him. The air was still, almost as though the world was holding its breath.

Harry stepped forwards and noticed that Jim held back, standing beside his vehicle. 'You okay?'

'Fine,' Jim said. 'It's just, well, I . . .' His voice broke off.

Harry understood. 'Just follow me, okay? And we'll deal with what we've got together.'

'Yeah, thanks,' Jim agreed, and he stepped in behind Harry as they walked towards the shore.

HARRY WAS SURPRISED to find that they were first on the scene. Usually, he'd arrive at something like this and the place would already be busy as hell, not only with PCSOs and uniformed officers, but detectives and the crime scene investigation team, or CSI as it was better known, as well. Not that the real-life CSI was anything like the shiny darkness portrayed on television. The team he was used to back in Bristol was run by a woman with all the charm and warmth of a walk-in freezer stuffed full with meat hung from the kind of hooks made famous by the film *A Texas Chainsaw Massacre*. She was cold, brutally so at times, and seemed to regard everyone, even God, Harry suspected, as beneath her. He wondered what he would be getting this time and also when they would arrive. So, he asked Jim.

'CSI? Not a clue. Don't think I've ever seen them called out if I'm honest.'

'Seriously?'

'Couldn't tell you the last time anything like this happened here,' Jim said.

Harry walked on, edging closer to the shore of the dark water before them. 'We don't know what happened so let's not go jumping to conclusions. Who put the call in?'

'Couple of wild swimmers apparently,' Jim said. 'They should still be here, right?'

'Should be is a whole world away from actually are,' said Harry. 'I've lost count of the number of times people have buggered off from a crime scene after reporting it. Seem to forget that they can actually be of help to an investigation.'

The sound of a car door opening then slamming shut cut through the air. It was followed by footsteps. Eventually, a figure came into view. It was a woman wearing what looked at first to be a huge wizard's cloak, but at closer inspection was some kind of large waterproof, fleece-lined robe which stretched all the way to her ankles. 'Are you the police?'

'That we are,' Harry said. 'And you are?'

'The person who reported it . . . *her* . . . the body.'

Harry heard the shock still wild and alive in the woman's voice. 'Perhaps you could show us where it is, then, madam, if that's okay?'

'Do I have to?'

'Well, it will stop us making a mess of a potential crime scene by tripping over it,' Harry said. 'And it'll save time as well. We need to secure and preserve the site.'

The woman, Harry could tell, didn't seem entirely sure that she wanted to comply with his request.

'Perhaps you can just show us?' Jim asked.

The woman nodded and raised an arm to point towards some thick brush just up from the lake and lying between it and the road which ran along its edge.

'We usually get changed in there, you see, or at least close by, to give a bit of extra cover. Not that anyone's going to see us, not now. But anyway, that's where we found her. When we came in from our swim.'

Harry was astonished. 'You mean you've already been out? In that?' He gestured towards the lake, its black surface looking even more foreboding than before. Just looking at it made him feel cold. Icily so. 'Why?'

'You don't wild swim, then?' the woman asked.

'I don't swim full stop,' Harry said. 'I mean, I can, but I don't choose to. Which is a sensible decision, I think. Not my kind of thing.'

'You don't know what you're missing,' the woman replied.

Dead bodies in the middle of the night for a start, Harry thought but kept it to himself.

'Forecast was for a clear night,' the woman explained. 'So, we decided a midnight swim would be good. And it wasn't until we came back in that we found . . .' Her voice broke off then.

'You swim in wetsuits?' Harry asked, working to keep the atmosphere as relaxed as possible, which wasn't easy. It was necessary though. Stress made people not think straight and right now he needed this woman and her friend, who he assumed was still in the car, thinking the straightest they had ever done in their whole life. These first few moments at a crime scene were vital.

'No, skins,' the woman replied.

'What naked?' Jim asked, his interest suddenly piqued. 'No way!'

The woman shook her head and smiled. 'No, skins, as in just our skin and a swimsuit. Though we do skinny dip occasionally.'

'So, there were just two of you swimming?' Harry asked.

'Yes, just us two,' the woman said. 'Myself and Ruth. I'm Cathy by the way.'

'We'll need to speak to you both,' Jim said then, and Harry could see that he'd left his uncertainty back with the Land Rover and was in police mode now. 'I'll have to take some details down, interview you at the station as well, but I'd like a chat now, if that's okay?'

Cathy gave a nod which Harry noticed was also partly a shiver. Why on earth would anyone go swimming at midnight in a freezing cold lake? He couldn't understand it at all. Absolute madness.

'You look cold,' Harry observed. 'If you could just show us exactly where the body is then we can make sure the site is secure, you can head back to your car to stay warm, and then PCSO Metcalf here will be over to talk to you in a few minutes. Does that sound okay?'

Cathy seemed to agree, giving another shivering nod of her head. Walking away from them she approached the area she had pointed at before. Harry's eyes had just about adjusted to the darkness by now and he was able to make things out a little better by the moonlight, which was bright and shone eerily on the world beneath it.

'Just over there,' Cathy said, raising a hand again to point. 'You can just make it, I mean her, out now.'

Harry narrowed his eyes and stared into the darkness. For a moment he saw nothing, but then he noticed it, a dark shape resting on the ground by a clump of small, windswept trees, which were rested on the shore, between the lake and the road.

'Thanks, Cathy, you've done really well. Now you get yourself back to your car and Jim here will be over in a moment, okay?'

With Cathy gone, Harry rested a hand on Jim's shoulder. 'You good with this?'

Harry heard him suck in a slow, deep breath. 'Aye,' he said. 'Let's get it done.'

And so together they walked a path to the dead.

CHAPTER FIFTEEN

As Harry walked with Jim towards the body, his torch beam swinging left to right, scanning the land in front of them for anything that might seem out of place, he was struck by how, even under the cover of darkness, the creeping dread of what they were doing grabbed hold of his stomach and gave it a royal twist, like a rope in the hands of an old sailor. As yet he hadn't shone the torch ahead to the body. It was a little habit of his, and he told himself it was to give a last moment of respect, though there was a sense of unease to it as well. He knew what was ahead, what was waiting for him, and he preferred to deal with that as he drew close rather than from a distance. Death didn't hide in the shadows. It simply was. And it waited for you in silence, Harry had always thought. It didn't matter if it was a blood-spattered kitchen, a bullet-ridden military Land Rover, or here and now beside a still lake in the dead of night, death was death. And Harry had always sensed that it was staring at him, daring him to challenge it, knowing that he couldn't, that he was helpless. Which was why he did the job in the first place, wasn't it, to prove to death that it wouldn't have the last laugh, that someone would be held to account?

Walking on in silence, Harry's thoughts turned even darker, dragging him away with shocking speed from where he was at that moment to a place so many years ago now that it shocked him how it still felt so fresh and new in his mind, a wound which refused to heal. Or was it that he just kept on picking at the scab?

He'd been on leave from the Paras. Tour over, it was time to visit home, check in on his mum and Ben. He'd had a rough time out in theatre, but then they all had, and it wasn't just his body that was exhausted, but in many ways his soul, too. War did that to you, Harry knew. No one was ever left unchanged by it. And then, what he had found on arrival at home, well that had changed him even more, and beyond all recognition.

He had arrived at the family home, an average 1990s three-bed house in the little market town of Frome in Somerset. The town itself had a few years left before it would become a mecca for hipsters and celebrities, but then, was nothing more than a tired place hankering after the memories of what it had been so many years before. The night had been cold and wet, with winter doing its best to chill Harry to the core. The roads were slick with rain.

The first thing which had struck Harry as off was that the front door had been hanging open, the rain sweeping in on the edge of a blustering wind dancing in the dark. The second had met him as soon as he had entered: a lounge turned upside down with broken furniture, a smashed television, photos from the walls now on the floor. But it was the blood which had drawn him. Not just that it was there at all, but the quantity of it, as though someone had come in and painted with it. Then he'd seen her, his mum, lying on the floor, and beside her, Ben, his younger brother, barely a teenager, unconscious.

Harry had called the police immediately, but he had known who was responsible for the carnage he'd found. And as he'd held the hand of his dying mother, cradling his younger brother in his arms, he'd known that the rest of his life would have but one purpose: to find the man responsible and to make him pay. And yet, nearly twenty years on, his father was still a free man, the case so cold it froze Harry's breath.

'This doesn't seem real,' Jim said, and Harry was ripped from his gloomy past to his dreary present, as they drew closer to the silhouette of the body just ahead of them. 'I mean, Sophie's only fifteen. She's just a kid! Who'd do something like this?'

'That's quite a leap you've taken,' Harry said, shaking his head to dislodge his thoughts of the past. 'We don't know it's Sophie. Not yet. Always need to keep an open mind. If you don't, you might miss something, not just in what you're seeing, but what you're thinking.'

The trouble was that Harry had already made the leap himself. He'd been mentally preparing himself for what they would find from the moment he'd received the call that a body had been found.

'No, you're right, sorry,' Jim said, slipping on a large pebble and stumbling a little. 'But with her being reported missing yesterday and now this, it's just, well, you know . . .'

Harry stopped and looked at Jim. 'Yes, I do know. So, I'm going to guess that this is a first for you, right?'

Jim said nothing but gave a slight nod.

'Best advice I can give is to just go with it, okay?' Harry

said. 'Whatever we find, whatever we see, our job is to give that person dignity and to do everything we can to find out what happened and why. Remain objective. Be observant. Don't look at anything and think it isn't important, because right now everything is.' Then he added, 'And just so you know, in case you're worried about it, I threw up when I hit my first crime scene that had a body. And I'd seen plenty of dead in the army, trust me.'

'Really?' Jim said. 'I just thought that you'd be fine with it. All that military experience, like.'

'There's a difference between the death of someone who's been trained to go into battle and someone who's had their life snatched away. Both are tragic, awful events, and I've lost more than a few mates in theatre. But murder, manslaughter, whatever it is, there's just something else about it.'

'Like what?'

Harry didn't know what to say to that. He'd tried to put his finger on it before and had never been quite able to. 'Sometimes,' he said, 'I think it's because I know it's down to me to find out who's responsible. Even though there's always a team, I still figure that it's still down to me and who that person was. Their lives, their family, friends, colleagues. It's what we do, right?'

'I guess,' Jim said. 'I'm just a PCSO, though.'

He'd started out simply by trying to help the lad feel okay about approaching a crime scene with a body, and ended up, as far as he could tell, talking more than a little bit of bollocks. 'No such thing as just a PCSO,' Harry said. 'I've not known you long, but you more than know what you're doing. You're thorough. You do the job because you care about the people here, right? So, no more of that horseshit, okay?'

'Yeah, okay,' Jim said, though Harry noticed that the reply wasn't exactly said with enormous conviction.

'First things first,' Harry explained, 'we look for anything that's out of place. We know there's a body up ahead, so we'll deal with that when we get there. Right now, we're trying to see if there's anything that could give us a clue as to how she was brought here and why.' He pulled out his phone. 'And it's always a good idea to take photos. Loads of them. A camera can sometimes pick something up that you haven't.'

Harry's torch was scanning the ground still but giving him nothing. This was the shore of a lake, and a pebbled one at that. They'd be lucky to find anything like a footprint, but it was always worth a look.

'Whoever brought her here would've parked up near the road,' Jim said. 'You can't drive down to here unless you want your car getting stuck.'

'Exactly,' Harry agreed. 'So, look for footprints, stones that look freshly turned or are pushed in deeper than those around them. Or something that's maybe fallen out of a pocket, been torn off. Anything.'

For the next few minutes, Harry and Jim skirted around the site, giving the body a wide berth of around ten metres, and taking photos of everything they possibly could. They found nothing. No footprints, no sign that anyone had been where they were now treading. Which was what Harry had expected, but it didn't take the edge off his disappointment.

With nothing found, Harry led the way over towards the body, then stopped. 'You got anything we can tape this area off with?'

'Shit, yes,' Jim said, his words hissing through his teeth. 'Sorry, should've grabbed it.'

'Just nip back and get it will you?' Harry instructed. 'I'll head on over to the body, you put a perimeter down. Right?'

Jim headed back to the car.

Alone now, Harry steeled himself for the final bit of the journey. These last few steps were always the most difficult and he'd made them often. But knowing what he was likely to find, a teenage girl who had had her whole life ahead of her, made it all so much worse.

With a slow, deep breath he edged forwards, still keeping his eyes on the ground, looking, always looking. The shore of the lake was a grey thing of pebbles and rocks, though down towards the water that all gave way, not to sand as such, but gravel.

At last, he was at the body, its feet pointing down towards the lake, its head resting against the softer grassier ground which led into the scrubland on the shore, between the lake and the road. And as he raised his torch beam to finally rest the bright light on it, Jim was back with him, the perimeter all set.

'Jesus Christ!' Jim said, staring at the body. 'That's not Sophie!'

'No,' Harry said. 'It isn't.'

It was Martha. Sophie's mum.

CHAPTER SIXTEEN

HARRY STARED AT THE TWO WOMEN IN FRONT OF HIM, who were leaning against the bonnet of their car, a red Vauxhall Astra, as he desperately tried to search for a way to begin questioning them, because right now he needed answers, and quickly. He had a missing teenager still not found, and now that same girl's mother lying on a bleak shoreline with her face pummelled in. If his boss had sent him north for the quiet life, then it was very clear that no one had informed the north of this quite yet.

He'd expected to find the body of a dead teenager. He had prepared himself for it. Had known that the following day would involve reporting the death to the parents, sitting them down to tell them the most godawful news in the world, news no parent should ever receive, period. That the day would then move into overdrive because there was child murder and if there was something that the press had a sixth sense for, it was that. No matter how hard you tried to put a lock on something like that, to stop the news getting out until a time when it was appropriate for it to be released, to protect the family, they always found out, and those sneaky, weaselly, greasy bastards would be all over it. But this wasn't that. Not by a long shot.

On seeing the body, Harry's emotions had been a mix of shock and relief. He'd chastised himself quietly for feeling such a way, as though one death was somehow less important than another, which it wasn't by any stretch of the imagination. And yet not finding Sophie's corpse waiting for them had, in a strange way, almost given him a sense of hope for the briefest of moments that she was okay. This had crumbled the moment he'd gone in for a closer look and seen the state of Martha's face, or what was left of it.

Lying on her back, Harry had found Martha's lifeless face staring up into a star-filled sky it would never see again, the left eye wide open, the right eye hidden somewhere in the gory mess. The right side of her face had been caved in, but not in a small way. It had been immediately clear to Harry that whoever had killed Sophie's mum had gone at the woman hard with something blunt and solid, pummelling her until she was almost unrecognisable. It was the kind of violence born of control lost, though the reason behind that was, at this moment, invisible to Harry. Although Martha's right eye socket was smashed in, Harry then spotted that her eye was still visible, but only as a blood-covered thing of mashed up jelly. The cheek was little more than fresh mince, and Harry was reminded of a steak tartare he'd once had in a posh restaurant, only this was one constructed from human flesh, weeping and seeping down onto the rocks and into the ground beneath. Her jaw was knocked so far to the left that it sat almost at right angles to the rest of her face, a gaping, ruined hole of broken teeth and blood, her lips almost torn off.

Harry had stood for a while, just taking it all in. The mess of Martha's face, the brutal nature of what had been done to her. And yet the rest of her looked peaceful almost. Harry would leave further investigation of the body to the CSI team and the pathologist, but from where he was standing the one odd thing about the whole scene was that there were no visible signs of a struggle at all, as though Martha had simply laid down on the ground and taken the beating. Which didn't make much sense, for a start. Not unless her assailant had taken her by surprise, but even so . . .

Leaning in for a closer look, Harry saw that the pebbles and rocks around Martha's left side had been disturbed. He didn't edge too close so as not to disturb the site, but it looked almost as though someone had stumbled or fallen near her. And that struck him as odd when the body itself was laid out so carefully. They were wet, too, for some reason.

Harry looked around and the light from his torch caught some broken branches and scuffed up, squashed grass in the scrubland Martha's head was rested against. It made sense, he thought, that if whoever had done this to her had slipped, then they would have probably tried to steady themselves against whatever their hands were lucky enough to find in the dark. One thing was really bothering Harry though, and that was simply how Martha got there in the first place. They'd only seen one car when they'd pulled in, and it belonged to Cathy and Ruth. So where was Martha's?

Harry pulled himself away from the awful images in his mind of what lay just beyond where he now stood with Jim, Ruth, and Cathy. Martha wasn't going anywhere, not yet anyway, and these two women clearly wanted and needed to get home.

'So,' Harry began, noticing that Jim had his PNB in his

hands, ready to take notes, 'Can we just take your names and contact details, please, for our records?'

'I'm Cathy,' the woman they had spoken to earlier said. 'Cathy Armstrong.'

'And I'm Ruth Arkwright,' the other woman said, then added, 'as in the TV show, *Open All Hours.*'

Jim looked to Harry. 'What show?'

'Don't worry about it,' Harry said. 'It was before my time as well.'

Cathy was no longer in her huge swimming robe. Both women were wearing fleece jackets and woolly hats, their hands clasped around metal mugs, which judging by the smell, were filled with hot chocolate. They both gave their addresses and telephone numbers, as well as email addresses.

'Can you just run through things for us,' Harry asked, keeping his voice calm and relaxed. 'From when you came to the lake to when you discovered the body.'

Although it was Cathy who Harry and Jim had met first, it was Ruth who spoke now.

'Cathy picked me up at eleven thirty,' she said. 'We both live in Middleham so it's about half an hour away, but we always give ourselves longer, what with faffing about and whatnot. You know what it's like.'

'And you came straight here?'

'Yes,' Ruth said. 'Not much open at that time of night, so no reason to stop.'

'Did you see or hear anything suspicious when you arrived, or when you went out for your swim?' Harry asked, ignoring Ruth's sarcasm.

'Suspicious?' Ruth asked. 'Like what?'

'Anything really,' Harry said. 'Something not quite

where it's meant to be, something that wasn't here the last time, something out of place?'

'Voices, perhaps?' Jim added.

Harry was already feeling like he was clutching at straws, but he had to start somewhere.

'Well, for a start, it was dark, like right now,' Cathy said. 'And we weren't looking for anything, so we didn't see anything.'

'Or hear anything,' Ruth added. 'That's why night swimming is so lovely because it's just so quiet.'

Harry noticed an edge to Cathy's voice. It was clear that they both wanted to get home. But he had a job to do.

'And you're sure there was nothing out of the ordinary?'

'No,' Ruth said, shaking her head. 'This is Semerwater in Wensleydale. The only thing out of the ordinary you'll find around here is someone making their tea the wrong way.'

'There's a wrong way?' Harry asked.

Cathy shook her head and rolled her eyes. 'Honestly, a word of advice; don't get her started.'

Harry quickly moved on, not wishing to be sidetracked. 'So, you arrived at the lake, got changed, and went for a swim. You didn't see anyone? No one hanging around by the lake or anything like that?'

'Not a soul,' Cathy said. 'It was just us, and that's the way we like it, isn't it, Ruth?'

Ruth gave a firm nod then drained the last of her hot chocolate.

Jim asked, 'Could the body have been there when you arrived, and you just didn't see it?'

'I suppose,' Ruth shrugged. 'We walked past where it is to get into the lake, but we weren't really looking, what with the pebbles being so sodding painful to walk on barefoot.'

'So,' Harry asked,' when your swim was finished, you came back in. What time would you think that was?'

Cathy and Ruth glanced at each other for a moment.

'We got here just after twelve,' Cathy said, 'and were in the water by twenty past. We swam for half an hour, so were out at just before one.'

'And that's when you found her?'

Ruth nodded. 'Who is she, by the way?'

'I'm afraid I can't say,' Harry said. 'I'm sure you understand.'

'How did you know the body was female?' Jim asked.

'We looked,' Cathy said, a hint of weary frustration in her voice. 'It wasn't that difficult to tell, despite all the blood on her face.'

Harry paused for a moment before speaking again. So far, they had learnt nothing. For all he knew the body had been dumped there earlier in the evening, and it was only bad luck on the part of the two swimmers that they'd found her. And if they hadn't, she could very easily have been there till the coming morning, which would only have made things worse, with a crime scene open to the elements for a whole night, animal interference, and goodness knew what else.

'Right,' Harry said at last, 'I think we're done here, for now anyway. However, I'm afraid that I will have to ask you both to come to the station tomorrow morning so we can go over everything again.'

Cathy was about to protest, but Harry held up a hand to stop her before she had a chance.

'Something may pop into your mind when you're heading home, or in the morning after you've slept. I'm sure you understand that we need to do everything we can to find out what happened.'

'Yes, of course,' Cathy said.

Ruth voiced her agreement, though it was somewhat lacking in enthusiasm, Harry noted.

'So, thanks for your time and for calling this in. You did the right thing.'

'What else would we do?' Cathy asked.

'You'd be surprised,' said Harry. 'Some people would have run from this and never turned back.'

'That's not how things work in the dales,' Ruth said.

'No, I'm beginning to see that.'

Ruth and Cathy turned around to get into their car, but Cathy turned back and looked over at Harry. 'You really need to try it sometime, you know,' she said. 'Wild swimming will change your life.'

Harry smiled as kindly as he could.

'I'm serious,' she said. 'It's beautiful. The feel of the water. Even the cold. And at night, it's not just the stars, but everything else. Lights from the houses way up on the fell. Cars driving around, their headlights just cutting through the night light laser beams. Honestly, you need to.'

Ruth laughed. 'Listen to you getting all poetic! And about the headlights of cars, too.'

Harry caught something then in what Cathy had said. 'Cars?'

Cathy nodded.

'So, you saw some when you were swimming?'

'Just a farmer,' Cathy said. 'They're often out at all hours, sorting out sheep or lambs or whatever.'

Harry wasn't so sure. 'What time was this?' He asked. 'Where?'

Cathy pointed back up the way that Jim had driven down earlier when he'd brought Harry to the lake.

'Headed off up there,' she said. 'Looked really arty as well. Wish I'd had my camera, those headlights sweeping through the dark. Amazing.'

Harry noticed Jim's eyes were on him now.

'What are you thinking?' Jim asked.

Harry wasn't sure, didn't want to comment, but his mind was working now, chewing over what they'd been told.

'If you were swimming out, then you wouldn't have seen a car coming down to the lake, would you?' Harry said, looking at Cathy and Ruth. 'But heading back to shore, that's a different story, isn't it?'

'Is it?' Jim asked.

Harry looked up towards the dark fells around them. If his gut was right, and it usually was in these matters, then there was every chance that Cathy and Ruth had seen Martha's murderer leaving the scene of the crime.

CHAPTER SEVENTEEN

'So how long are we going to have to wait?' Harry asked as Cathy and Ruth headed off back down the dale to Middleham. 'Until the crime scene team turn up, I mean?'

For the first time since they'd arrived, Harry was starting to feel the chill in the night air. He was tempted to head back to the Land Rover to get warmed up.

Jim glanced down at his watch. 'Half an hour, give or take. You fancy a coffee?'

Harry sparked up at this. 'You never mentioned you'd brought coffee.'

'It's the middle of the night,' Jim said. 'I figured something strong and sweet would be a good idea. Though I realise now you probably hate it like that. Sorry. Should've asked.'

Harry beamed at Jim. 'It's coffee,' he said, 'that's all that matters. Coffee! Grab it now, before the next yawn I do threatens to suck in that lake.'

Jim jogged over to his vehicle, returning with a battered stainless-steel flask and a couple of tin mugs.

'Here you go,' he said, handing one of the mugs to Harry before pouring the coffee out.

Harry stared at the milky brown liquid swirling around in his mug and sucked in the wonderful, rich, earthy smell of it. And to think he'd thought that all they drank up here was tea!

Harry took a sip and the taste of the coffee, the sweet rich milky goodness of it, shot through him like a jolt of electricity. 'Bloody hell,' he said, 'that's lush!'

'Aye, it is that,' Jim said. 'Most folks drink tea, as you've probably noticed, but I'm partial to a nice brew of coffee, too. So, this is freshly ground. None of that instant muck.'

Harry could have hugged him. At crime scenes the coffee, if there even was any in the first place, was usually little more than piss in a cup, a weak brown liquid that burned and scalded and made your breath stink like a geography teacher's at the end of a bad week yelling at teenagers. But this right now? It was proper coffee. The kind he would make for himself at the weekend. Sunday morning coffee.

With the coffee getting to work and firing the caffeine and sugar through his body, Harry thought back over what they'd found and what they knew. Which, he had to admit, was sod all. Sophie was missing, her mum was dead, most likely murdered, but why or by whom he hadn't the faintest idea, and the only witnesses to anything so far were two outdoor swimmers who didn't see anything other than some headlights. But then it was very, very early in the day, quite literally too, Harry thought, so something would turn up. It always did.

'I'm going to take a wander around,' Harry said. 'Best you stay here by the crime scene, Jim, just in case the CSI bunch turn up and need directing. That okay?'

'No worries,' Jim said. 'Anything you're looking for in particular?'

'I'm not sure yet,' Harry said, and with his coffee mug in hand, turned and walked away.

The first thing Harry did was take a wander up the lane away from the way they'd driven in. It led off past a farm and then on up the side of a hill. Turning around after a few minutes he had a better view of the lake and was, for the first time, struck by its presence. When he'd first seen it, the lake had been simply a crime scene in his mind, but up here it took on something else entirely. It was a black mirror, the surface as glass and reflecting the stars above, though for a moment Harry felt as though he was looking down through a window, a hole or a portal perhaps, and into another place completely. Perhaps Jim's feelings towards the place weren't exactly misplaced, Harry thought, because there was an otherworldly feel to it, an eeriness of being watched, of deep history mooching around the shoreline to sink beneath its depths.

Harry walked back down the lane, passing the lake on his left, and towards the bridge they'd crossed when they'd arrived. The coffee had certainly warmed him as well as woken him up, not least because he was able to clasp the metal mug in his hands and enjoy the heat from it, swapping them over every few minutes so that he could hold his torch in his free hand.

Passing the area of bushes and small trees, Harry's eyes were scanning the area as best they could, hoping to find something that was off or out of place. Nature didn't do perfect lines, so in a place like this, he was always looking for something that didn't quite fit, be that a straight line or a curve. As with most roads and lanes, Harry found some odds and ends scattered along its edge, including a crushed and crumpled can of long gone iced coffee, a couple of wooden lollipop sticks, a bicycle clip, an empty bottle of supermarket vodka, and a weathered, torn condom pouch. Harry thought how all those things together certainly combined to form an interesting evening of entertainment, but as to evidence of what had happened at the lake over the last few hours, they didn't amount to much at all. Still, he took photos of it all then bagged it up to give to the CSI team when they arrived. They'd undoubtedly complain that he'd been rummaging around a crime scene, but that's what you got for trying to be helpful.

Harry arrived at the bridge, walked over, turned around, and headed back to the lake. The CSI team would be arriving any time and he really wanted to be there when they did. Not that he thought Jim would be rubbish at dealing with them, far from it actually, but simply because he wanted to make sure he was fully involved in what was going on and could talk through with them what he and Jim knew so far.

Walking back up the lane, the lake now on his right, Harry strode past the scrubland again, only this time something caught his eye. He stopped, backtracked, and slowly allowed the beam from his torch to trace a white line of discovery in the dark. And there in front of him, buried deep in the bushes, he found it: Martha's car.

'Jim!' Harry called out. 'Jim, mate! Over here! Now!'

The sound of racing footfalls came to Harry then from the darkness ahead and a few moments later Jim oozed out of it. 'What's up? What've you found?'

Harry gestured with a nod of his head. 'See for yourself,' he said, then cast the light of his torch over the car once again.

'Interesting place to park,' Jim said.

'You got another pair of gloves in the Land Rover?' Harry asked. 'I fancy a closer look.'

Jim dashed back up the lane and returned carrying what Harry had requested, including some for himself.

Jim handed Harry a pair of gloves. 'Shouldn't we wait for the CSI team?'

'I've waited long enough,' Harry growled back. 'There's a dead woman for them to be getting on with and they don't seem to be in any particular hurry about it. So, having a look around this isn't going to do anyone any harm, is it?'

Harry had a quick look at the ground to try and get an idea as to how or why Martha had parked her car where it now was. It was clear from the tracks in the dirt, leading off the road and into the bushes, that others had parked in the same place before Martha's car had turned up there. Harry had a fairly good idea as to the reasons why anyone would need to hide away so well from prying eyes, and the sordid nature of it was, he was pretty sure, not the kind of thing that Martha, or indeed George, who he'd met the day before, would have anything to do with. They just didn't strike him as the dogging type.

At the vehicle, Harry and Jim circled it, pushing their way through the bushes as carefully as possible, always looking to see if they could find anything. With nothing coming to light, other than the fact that it was clear from the broken branches, and the numerous tyre tracks on the ground, that it was regularly used as a parking place, Harry opened the driver's door. The car was clean, he noticed. Spotless almost, much like the house he'd walked around, and areas on the dashboard looked damp. He shone his light under the driver's chair, looked into the pockets in the door, then went on to check the passenger seat and still nothing. Opening the rear door, all that he noticed there was some black grease rubbed off on the otherwise clean carpet, though what it could have been from he couldn't guess, and a box. He dragged it over and opening it found six bottles of wine staring back up at him. He pulled one out to read the label only to discover that it wasn't a decent Rioja, but communion wine. Martha really was religious, wasn't she? he thought.

'Anything round your side?' Harry called out to Jim as he stepped back, shutting the door.

'This,' Jim said, startling Harry a little as he appeared next to him rather than calling from where Harry had expected him to be.

Harry shone his light over to what Jim had in his hands.

'I reckon this is Sophie's,' Jim said, holding out his left hand. 'I mean, we saw the phone Martha had herself, yesterday, so I doubt this is hers. Anyway, why would she have two?'

It was a smartphone, and not a cheap one either, in a bejewelled pink protective case.

Harry reached out for it and hit the power button. The phone lit into life but presented him with a request for a fingerprint to gain access. 'Plastic bag?' Harry asked.

Jim held one out and Harry popped it inside.

'What about this stuff?' Jim asked, and held out his right hand.

Harry looked down to see a pair of sunglasses, an air freshener, two worship CDs, and a paper bag.

'What's in the bag?' Harry asked.

'Pills,' Jim said. 'A few boxes, not that I know what any of it is.'

'Might be something, might be nothing,' Harry said at

which point he noticed flashing blue lights blinking in the darkness somewhere beyond where they were now stood.

'CSI,' Jim said turning towards the lights, which were growing brighter as they drew closer.

'And about bloody time,' Harry agreed. 'We need Martha's identity confirmed before we can go and deliver the notification of death to George.'

'Shit, yes, that,' Jim said. 'Shit . . .'

Harry caught the worry in Jim's voice. 'Don't worry, it won't be for you to do,' he said. And with the phone in its plastic bag now stuffed into his pocket, he led the way back out of the bushes.

CHAPTER EIGHTEEN

WITH THE ARRIVAL OF THE CSI TEAM, AND THEN AN ambulance sometime later, the shore of Semerwater took on a depressingly sinister air. To Harry it seemed as though the night itself was skulking around the surrounding hills, closing everything else off, and just staring down at what was happening, pushing in with even more darkness. It was oppressive and he longed for the dawn.

A white tent was erected over the body and the pathologist had got to work, wearing a white paper suit of personal protective equipment, or PPE, like the rest of the CSI team. Harry had always thought that this gave them a ghoulish air, white ghosts stalking the place where a death had occurred.

Jim had been sent off to knock on the doors of the few surrounding farms and houses on the off chance that the residents would have seen or heard something. It was a long shot, that was for sure, thought Harry, who had handed over the stuff he'd found on the road to one of the CSI team, and received a grumble in return.

Matt Dinsdale had arrived at around the same time and, much to his clearly expressed annoyance, so had Detective Superintendent Swift, seeing as Matt had given him a lift. He'd stayed over in Hawes for the night rather than go home and, Harry noticed as soon as he'd seen the superior officer, had a look in his eyes that could cut through steel. Harry decided to not ask why it had taken them so long to arrive, considering that Matt and the DSup had no further to travel than he and Jim, because it was clear from the off that Swift was not in the best of spirits.

'I'm hoping, DCI Grimm,' Swift had said on meeting him at the shore, 'that this isn't a sign of things to come.'

'How do you mean?' Harry had asked.

The DSup had drilled his eyes into him then and leaned in real close to hiss his answer. 'That you've not traipsed up here with a load of shit on your shoes.'

Harry had gone to answer, but the DSup had held up a condescending finger to shush him before he'd even begun. 'I know you're a troublemaker,' the DSup had said. 'The kind of person who has a gravitational pull when it comes to crime and the scum who commit it. So, let me make something clear going forward: I'll not stand for it, you hear? Things are quiet around here, and safe. And although whatever has happened here has nothing to do with you at all, it strikes me as an ominous sign indeed that your arrival was just a couple of days ago. Do not be an omen of ill fortune, Grimm. Do you hear?'

Harry had allowed the DSup his moment, giving no backchat, no repost, and when Swift had calmed down, had instead, simply filled him in on what he and Jim had found and what they'd done.

'Well,' Swift said, 'at least there's nothing to complain

about with your knowledge of police procedure. Which is something.'

'And you're sure it's Martha?' Matt asked.

'Have to wait for the pathologist and the rest of the CSI team to confirm that,' Harry said. 'But yes, I'm sure.'

For a moment Matt said nothing, but when he did, his voice was sombre and quiet. 'This is going to kill George, you know. He can't do anything without her.'

Harry said, 'He must be wondering where she is though. Has he called it in himself yet, that she's not at home?'

'No reports of it,' Matt said. 'Maybe she sneaked out or something?'

'And why the hell would she do that?' Harry asked, immediately realising his words had come out harsher than he had meant them to.

'I don't know,' Matt said, stuffing his hands deep into his pockets. 'Just trying to think around what's happened, that's all.'

'She was here for a reason,' Harry said, 'but what that reason was, I've no idea.'

'Sophie?' Matt asked.

Harry shook his head. 'I can't see this being a place she'd either end up, or somewhere she'd arrange to meet her mum, can you? And why do it in the middle of the night? Doesn't make sense. None of it does.'

'Poor bastard,' Matt muttered. 'A missing daughter and a dead wife. How do you cope with that?'

Harry had nothing. In a situation like this, no one ever did.

'Ah,' Swift said, having stayed on the periphery of Harry and Matt's conversation, 'here comes the pathologist now. I'll introduce you, Grimm. Follow me.'

Harry dropped in behind the DSup as he moved off to meet the figure approaching them from the direction of the crime scene.

'Brace yourself,' Matt said.

'Why?' Harry asked.

'You'll see.'

'DCI Grimm, this is Rebecca Sowerby, the pathologist.'

The woman in front of Grimm pulled back the hood on her white PPE suit, pulled her mask up onto her forehead, then snapped off her rubber gloves.

Harry reached out with his right hand, but she didn't take it and made a point of the fact by stuffing her hands in her jacket pockets. 'You the officer in charge?'

The pathologist's voice had a tone to it that Harry recognised, as did her bearing, which was upright, forceful, and gave the immediate impression that she was used to being in charge. Whether she was military or not, he wasn't sure, but she had all the markings of an officer he would have hated. Not that Harry was quick to jump to conclusions, it was just that his gut was a good judge of people. And it was telling him that here was someone he was probably best avoiding for the rest of his life.

'I was first on the scene,' Harry replied.

'Well, it's a shit show, isn't it?'

'Bollocks is it,' Harry said, responding in kind. 'Perimeter is set, crime scene is undisturbed. Job done.'

Sowerby sneered and Harry's mouth went thin with anger.

The pathologist turned to Swift. 'Where did you find this one, then?'

'He was sent, not found.'

'Send him back.'

Harry bristled at this. 'We secured the site, touched nothing, left it for you. If you wanted it done differently, you should've arrived quicker.'

Sowerby was back on Grimm, ripping off the end of his sentence like a piece of meat. 'And how was I supposed to do that, seeing as I've just driven here in the middle of the night from one arse end of nowhere to another?'

'On that witch's broom you've clearly got shoved up your arse,' Harry said.

'Grimm!' Swift bellowed, for the first time deciding to be a part of the conversation. 'Who the hell do you think you are to talk to anyone like that, never mind Miss Sowerby!'

Harry stared at the woman as she shook her head in frustration, though there was a hint of a smile threatening the corner of her mouth. Was she always like this? he wondered. Because there was nothing at all wrong with what he and Jim and done, and he should know, seeing as he'd done too many crime scenes to mention. Unless, of course, this became a pissing contest, and then he'd roll them out quick as you like.

'What did you find?' Harry asked.

'What do you think we found?' Sowerby asked. 'A tap-dancing mule? A class of students on a geography field trip?'

Harry had nothing to say and simply allowed the pathologist the time and space to say whatever it is she wanted to say because it was clear that she was going to say it anyway.

'The deceased is a woman in her mid-to-late forties. Cause of death was having the right side of her head caved in. With what, I'm not sure yet, but I'll be able to tell more when I get her back and on a slab. There are plenty of blood-spattered rocks around her so we're taking those with us to see which matches. And also in the hope that we find some fingerprints. Unsurprisingly, this isn't the best of places to carry out a full examination of a corpse.'

'Time of death?' Swift asked.

'I'd say within the last two or three hours, give or take,' Sowerby answered. 'Most of the damage was done with her lying on the ground. No sign of a struggle, no defensive wounds or anything that I could see. I reckon the first blow knocked her unconscious, then she was finished off good and proper once she fell.'

'Can you confirm her identity?' Matt asked. 'We need to tell the husband. Their daughter's missing as well.'

Harry noticed Sowerby raise an eyebrow at this, though whether or not that was her showing a touch of empathy he wasn't sure.

'We found a purse under her body,' Sowerby said. 'Cards and photos and the undamaged side of her face confirm her as Martha Hodgson.' She turned her attention to Matt. 'So, are you the poor bastard who has to give the news? Shittiest job on earth if you ask me.'

Matt was about to speak, but Harry stepped in. 'I'll do that,' he said, and he noticed a look of mild surprise on Swift's face.

'Well, rather you than me,' Sowerby said. 'We also found some fresh tyre marks at the other end of the shore, near the bridge, and footprints leading to and from them, to the body. Looks like someone left in a bit of a hurry. She must have really pissed someone off to have that done to her.'

'What about the car?' Harry asked. 'The one in the bushes?'

'The one you had a look over before we turned up? That one, you mean?'

Harry was quickly moving from disliking Rebecca

Sowerby to hoping he'd at some point in his life have a chance to feed her to a bear.

'We got bored,' Harry said with a shrug. 'You know how it is. And we figured it would be fun to make your life difficult.'

'Well, we found fingerprints, namely ones belonging to the deceased, and those of three other individuals.'

'Three?'

'You worried you can't count that high?'

'Cars usually have loads of prints in them,' Harry said, resisting the urge to bite back. 'Friends given lifts, mechanics . . .'

'Most cars haven't been wiped on a weekly basis to keep them spotless,' Sowerby said. 'And that one hasn't just been regularly cleaned, it's been wiped down tonight. It's still damp in places, which I'm sure you noticed, too, being a detective. So the prints are probably from the husband and daughter, and someone else.'

'Cars aren't spotless,' Harry pressed. 'That's just weird.'

'Well, we're taking the car with us for a proper going over,' Sowerby added. 'See what else we can find, if anything. Shine a black light through it as well, just on the off chance it picks something up.'

Harry laughed at this. 'A black light? You expecting to find that the car's been wiped clean because Martha was out at night stuffing it full with murder victims, and what we have here is revenge from a relative?'

Matt stared at Harry. 'What, you mean you think that's what happened? Hells bells, this is a proper crime, isn't it? And in Wensleydale! Good job I got my detective quali-fication!'

Harry rested his left hand on Matt's shoulder. 'I'm

kidding,' he said, trying to not smile. 'So, calm down, yeah? Ease back a bit from the serial killer idea.'

Sowerby said, 'Anyway, you'll have the prints, and any other evidence we find, later on, once we've got it all together, along with my report after I've had a proper look at the body. Now, if it's all the same with you, I'll be getting home.'

She didn't even wait for goodbyes and instead just turned on her heels and headed off, away from Harry, Matt, and the DSup.

'She's a real charmer,' Harry said to no one in particular. 'Which circle of Hell did you find her on?'

'We'll talk about this tomorrow,' Swift said. 'But suffice it to say, Grimm, I am not happy. Not happy at all.'

Matt, Harry saw, was just standing there shaking his head. 'Doesn't make sense,' he said.

'What doesn't?' Harry asked.

'Any of it,' Matt replied. 'Sophie going missing, is one thing, but all of this? What the hell does it all mean? Why would her mum be murdered? Who'd do that? Nothing like this ever happens around here. It just doesn't.'

Harry heard footsteps behind him and turned to see Jim approaching.

'Anything?'

Jim shook his head. 'No one heard or saw anything,' he said. 'Only thing I can confirm is that those headlights the two swimmers saw, well, they weren't from any of the local farms. No one's been out. It's been a quiet night.'

Harry sucked in a deep breath and turned to the DSup. 'If it's okay with you, Sir, I'll head off and see Mr Hodgson. I think it's best I get that done now. No point waiting.'

Swift gave a nod of approval and with a look at Matt headed off.

'I'll come with you, Harry,' Jim said. 'To see George, I mean.'

'You sure?' Jim gave a nod. 'He knows me. It'll maybe make it easier.'

'Nothing makes this easier,' Harry said. 'Nothing at all.'

CHAPTER NINETEEN

As Jim drove them back into Hawes, Harry checked the time. It was five-thirty in the morning, and he'd had approximately one hour's sleep in the last twenty-four hours. He'd survived for longer on less. Back in the Paras, sleep deprivation was part of the training, being pushed to the limit and then through it to see just how you would cope. He remembered being on one exercise, which had been comprised of little more than two days of digging trenches, a day of being shot at while manning the trenches, then two further days of filling the trenches back in. He was pretty sure he didn't sleep for the whole week. The tiredness had become so bad that some of the lads had started to hallucinate. Harry himself had been on sentry duty at one point and with the need to sleep so bad by that point he'd passed out on his feet, dropped to his knees, and only narrowly avoided impaling himself on his bayonet. Fun times.

Harry saw that Jim was yawning as well, and he couldn't stop the involuntary response of joining in.

The day was breaking from a black night into a grey

morning. It had been bright and sunny the day before, but it seemed to Harry that the weather had got wind of what had taken place in the dales below and decided to wear something more appropriate. The sky was slate grey, the air damp with the promise of rain, and the hills which had been so clear surrounding Hawes the day before were now shadowy spectres which would appear on occasion through wisps of low cloud.

Jim pulled the Land Rover up against the curb rather than driving up onto the driveway of the Hodgson's house.

For a moment or two, both Harry and Jim sat in silence, staring into the middle distance.

'I'll take the lead on this,' Harry said, rubbing his face with his hands to try and get some life into him and wake himself up a little.

'You sure?' Jim asked. 'I'm local, George knows me.'

'That's all true,' Harry said, 'but I'm the DCI. I'm not pulling rank, it's just the way this should be done. And like I said, I've done this before. That doesn't make it any easier, it just means I know what to expect.'

'So, what do I do?' Jim asked.

Harry could tell that he wanted to be useful. 'You'd be amazed at how important a decent mug of tea is at a time like this,' Harry said. 'And no, I'm not joking. It gives everyone something else to focus on, something to keep them busy. So as soon as we're in, I want you on with that if that's okay.'

'If you're sure.'

'Oh, I am,' Harry said. 'And one more thing, in cases like this? Most often, the murder was committed by a family member.'

Jim shook his head. 'No way Sophie did it.'

'I wasn't talking about Sophie.'

Jim's eyes went wide. 'George? No way. You've met him! He couldn't hurt a fly! And I mean literally couldn't, because he's weaker than a service station cup of tea!'

'I know,' Harry said, 'but George is a suspect. Though we won't say that as such, just enquire as to his whereabouts, okay?'

Jim gave a nod.

A couple of minutes later, Harry was stood with Jim at the Hodgson's front door. The time was now edging towards six and the day was fully awake now. He could hear sheep on the wind, their distant baaing the haunting sound of a time long since past and yet, here in Wensleydale, somehow still hanging on.

'Ready?' Harry asked and pressed the doorbell.

The sound of a faint chime from inside the house bounced back at them. Harry gave it a minute or two to see if there was any sound of movement from inside then pressed again. This time he heard a scuffle and then footsteps from somewhere above in the house. The footsteps drew closer until finally, the door opened.

Harry sucked in a deep breath, using it to keep himself calm, steady. 'Mr Hodgson?'

The man seemed even smaller and weaker than when Harry had met him the previous day. His eyes were sunk deep, his skin pale. If he'd slept at all, then it hadn't done much good. He'd clearly been up for some time, and busy, too, Harry thought, as George had his sleeves pulled up and there was sweat on his brow.

'Is this about Sophie? You've found her? I need to call Martha!'

'Can we come in?'

For a moment, George looked confused, his brow

furrowing and his deep-set eyes scrunching up. 'Of course,' George said. 'Is everything okay? Where's Sophie? Where is she? Have you found her? Please tell me you've found her!'

Harry moved past George and into the house, noticing as he did so marks on George's arms, a few bruises, and some cuts and grazes.

'I'm very clumsy,' George smiled. 'Gardening is my passion, but I'm always cutting and catching and knocking myself. You know how it is.' George pulled his sleeves down to cover his arms.

'It's a beautiful garden,' Harry said, then added, 'I think it best if we have a sit-down.' He then looked over to Jim. 'You mind sorting us all out some tea?'

'Oh, I'll do that, officer,' George said. 'Not a problem. Honestly, it isn't.'

'That's very kind,' Harry said, 'but I think it's best if we let Jim crack on with that so that you and I can talk. The lounge is through here, right?'

Harry made his way into the room from the hallway as Jim scuttled off to the kitchen.

In the lounge, Harry waited to sit down, not wishing to presume anything. But George came in and offered him a seat.

'If this is about Sophie,' George said, 'then I should give Martha a call. She leaves the house early every day, sometimes as early as five am would you believe, so I don't generally see her till later. She would want to be here, I'm sure. It won't take long.'

As George made to rise from his chair, Harry raised a hand to stall him. 'George, I'm here about Martha.'

George sat down again. Harry wasn't sure if the man was

growing paler by the moment or if it was just the bleakness of the day seeping in through the windows.

'Something's wrong, isn't it?' George said. 'Has there been a car accident? Is Martha okay?'

Harry took another long, deep breath. 'I have some very bad news I must tell you,' he said, the words sounding stilted to his own ears, but it was a well-practised line and he stuck with it because it ensured that he got the news across as clearly and succinctly as possible. 'We believe your wife, Martha, was involved in an incident at Lake Semerwater last night and I'm sorry to tell you that she was killed.'

There, the words were out, Harry thought, in no way relieved at all. He went to continue, but George got in first. 'Last night? Are you sure? But Martha was here I'm sure of it. She never goes out at night!'

Jim entered the lounge carrying a tray and put it down on the coffee table: three mugs of strong tea and some rich tea biscuits, the holy sacrament of bad news, Harry thought.

'I'll just nip back and get the sugar,' Jim said.

Harry pulled out his phone and showed a couple of pictures to George. One was of Martha's car, the other of the number plate.

'Yes, that's Martha's car,' George said. 'Where is it?'

'It's been taken away for further examination,' Harry explained. 'It was found at Semerwater. We think your wife drove there to meet someone, there was an argument or something, and your wife was killed. I am deeply sorry that this has happened, Mr Hodgson.'

George stood up. 'I'm going to call Martha now,' he said. 'Put an end to this nonsense. Just a minute, please.'

As George made to leave, he found Jim returning from

the kitchen with the sugar. 'Mr Hodgson? Where are you going?'

'To call my Martha,' George replied. 'Now, excuse me, please, Jim, there's a good lad.'

Jim didn't move an inch. 'Listen, George,' he said. 'Please, you need to sit down. I was with Harry. We found Martha together. It's her. She's dead, George. I'm so sorry.'

Harry watched as Jim gently guided George back to the sofas before sitting down next to him. 'Here,' Jim said, reaching out for a mug of tea and passing it to George.

'This doesn't make sense,' George said, cradling the mug in his hands. 'She can't be dead. Who would kill her? She can't be dead! She's my wife! She's a good person! What about Sophie? Oh, Martha . . .'

Harry decided it was best to allow George this moment and kept quiet as he saw tears begin to fall down the man's face.

A few minutes later, Harry decided it was time to ask a few gentle questions.

'George, I need to ask you a few things,' Harry said.

George nodded, sipped his tea. 'Yes, no problem. I understand.'

'First, can you tell me where you were last night, around the hours of eleven to one in the morning?'

'I was here!' George said. 'I did my podcast and then went to bed!'

'When was the last time you saw your wife?'

'Last night,' George said. 'When she took herself off to her, I mean our, bedroom.'

Harry noticed a pained flicker of movement on George's face though why he wasn't sure.

'What time was that?'

'Around nine I think,' George said. 'She was very tired with the Sophie thing.'

'You didn't go to bed together?'

George shook his head and there was that look again.

'I was doing my podcast, so I stayed up later.'

'And you didn't notice Martha leave the house last night? Or that she was gone at all at any point?'

George shook his head. 'Why would I?'

'Then I assume you're a heavy sleeper?' Harry said. 'To hear nothing at all, I mean.'

'Look,' George said at last, sitting further forward now, 'if you must know, we don't sleep in the same bedroom. We haven't for many years.'

Harry noticed a flicker of something across George's face then. Was it hurt? Regret? Both? Or something else. He didn't know, but he was pretty sure that George was sharing with them a situation he was none too pleased with.

'It's not as uncommon as you may think,' George continued. 'Martha rises early for work, so it means I don't get disturbed. And she really needs her sleep as well, so I don't want to go keeping her awake by tossing and turning. We're not young anymore, are we? And there's more to a relationship than the bedroom.'

Harry noticed that George was talking about his wife in the present tense. Most people did in situations like this. It was a difficult adjustment to make, and certainly not one to be made in the first few minutes after receiving the news.

Harry sipped his tea. It wasn't a bad cuppa, either. 'Have you noticed anything unusual about your wife's behaviour lately?'

'What are you implying?'

'I'm not implying anything,' Harry said. 'I'm simply

trying to find out as much as I can about what happened so that we can find the person responsible.'

'Then no, I haven't,' George snapped. 'Martha was very worried about Sophie. She was exhausted. She went to bed.'

'You must have been tired, too,' Jim said.

'Yes, of course,' George said, 'but my church podcast is important. People depend on me doing it, particularly those who can't get to church for whatever reason. It's an important ministry.'

Harry remembered something then and reached into his pocket. 'Do you recognise this?'

Inside a plastic bag hanging from Harry's hand was the pink phone he had found in Martha's car.

Harry saw that Jim was about to say or ask something so shut him up with a quick shake of his head.

'No,' George said, staring at it. 'Should I?'

'Found it in Martha's car,' Harry said. 'Thought it might be Sophie's.'

At this, George laughed, though the sound was cheerless. And Harry could see that he genuinely didn't recognise it.

'She's had so many different phones and covers,' he said. 'A parent can't be expected to remember them all!'

'So, this could be Sophie's?' Harry asked. 'You're just not sure.'

'I suppose it could, yes,' George said.

'If it is,' Harry continued, 'can you think of a reason as to why it would be in Martha's car and not with Sophie?'

'No, I can't,' George said, the words sharp.

Harry sensed that his questioning was now beginning to tax the man a little too much. Time to back off. If he needed to ask more questions, he could come back again. He stuffed the phone back into his pocket then rested his now empty mug back on the tray.

'I think that'll do for now, Mr Hodgson,' Harry said. 'I need to ask though if you have any friends or relatives who can come round and be with you right now? I don't want to leave you on your own, not at a time like this.'

George looked thoughtful for a moment, as though he was wrestling with a particularly difficult crossword question. 'I'm not sure, I can't think of anyone right now who could come round. I'll be fine, I'm sure.'

Jim stood up. 'It's okay, I'll stay,' he said. 'Make sure he's got some folk to come over.'

George made to protest but Harry quashed it, standing up as he spoke. 'Good,' he said. 'That's settled then. I'll be off to continue with our investigations. And any news I have, I'll be in touch.'

The three men walked from the lounge to the front door.

'Again, I'm so sorry to have given you this news,' Harry said, looking at George. 'With Sophie missing as well, you really do need friends and relatives for support. And we'll be sending a family liaison officer around as well, to see what other support we can provide at this difficult time.'

George nodded his thanks, then turned back into the house as Harry made to leave, Jim following him for a few steps.

'Harry? About that phone,' Jim asked.

'I know,' Harry said. 'Slipped my mind is all. Didn't realise I still had it. Don't worry about it.'

'Okay,' Jim said. 'And would you mind giving Gordy a buzz?'

Harry was about to ask why, but then the penny

dropped. 'You're kidding me, right? She's the family liaison officer?'

'Yep,' Jim said. 'See you later, Harry.'

Then Jim was back inside the house, the door shut behind him, and Harry walked off into the rest of his day, lifting his phone to his ear to punch in the call.

CHAPTER TWENTY

THE DAY HAD JUST DRIFTED PAST NOON WHEN HARRY woke. Having left the Hodgson's house, and called Gordy, he'd decided it was best if he just let the tiredness in his bones have its way for a while. So, he'd headed back to his room, leaving a message with Matt Dinsdale that he would be at the police room at the community centre early afternoon. Tiredness was okay up to a point, but after that, Harry knew he was next to no good at all, and on a case like this, he needed to be sharp.

Hunger was the first thing on Harry's mind, his stomach rumbling as he sat up on the edge of his bed. It was too late now for the rather splendid breakfast he'd enjoyed the previous morning, so he figured the best thing to do was to grab something en route.

Outside, the grey day was edging towards a darker shade now and the brightness of June was being replaced with the feel of late autumn. Harry pulled his coat in tight and dashed across the cobbles into Cockett's. On his right sat the butcher's counter, so Harry turned to the left to find the baker staring back.

'Hello, Love, can I help?' The woman facing him was all smiles.

Harry glanced at his watch. 'Missed breakfast,' he said. 'What do you suggest?'

'That you don't miss breakfast,' the woman smiled back. 'Most important meal of the day!'

'I could do with something warm if you've got anything,' Harry asked, looking briefly out through the shop window, rain now starting to dot its way across the glass.

'We've got bacon butties if you fancy,' the woman said. 'Bacon's cured by us. And we've pies and pasties.'

Harry looked at the pies. 'Pork and black pudding?'

'My favourite! One or two?'

Harry held up his index finger.

'That's not enough though, surely,' the woman said. 'How about some cake to be going on with?'

'Do I have to eat it with cheese?'

The woman laughed. 'Couple of slices?'

Harry then thought about the team who he'd be meeting up with in a few minutes. 'Make it a whole cake,' he said. 'And no, it's not all for me.'

Shopping done, Harry left Cockett's and walked up towards the main part of town, the rain chasing him onwards. He spotted Cunningham's on the left and remembered the conversation the previous night he'd had with Jenny about running. Perhaps later, he thought, and turned away to cross the road, dodging between a few cars rolling on through.

On entering the community centre, and then moving on through to the police room, Harry found that the team had been getting on with a few things since they'd all last met.

The furniture had been moved around to create a couple of workstations, each with a laptop and a couple of chairs, while just away from them a circle of chairs had been placed around one of the boards on the wall.

Matt was first to greet Harry as he entered the room. 'How do, Harry,' he said. 'You've bought cake? Good lad! Cheese?'

'Sorry, no,' Harry said.

'I'll get the kettle on.'

Harry handed Matt the cake then moved across to have a look at the board.

'What do you think?'

Harry turned to see Detective Constable Blades standing beside him.

'Not bad,' Harry said. 'Not bad at all.'

'All my own work,' Jenny said. 'We've not got much to go on yet, but I've put up there everything we do have. It's awful, isn't it? I mean, really terrible. Poor Martha.'

Harry nodded that it was indeed awful while looking through what was on the board. So far, there were three individuals mentioned, with Martha as deceased, Sophie as missing, and George as the relative. Various notes were around the names, along with some photos of the crime scene courtesy of Jim, Harry guessed, having followed his cue to record everything he could the night before.

'So, what have we got, then, Harry?' It was Matt again, but Harry sensed others were with him and turned to see that the detective sergeant had been joined by the two PCSOs, Jim and Liz.

'Where's Gordy?' Harry asked. 'Still with George?'

'No,' Jim said. 'She's been called down dale to something. George has a couple of friends round now.'

'Who?'

'Dave Calvert,' Jim said. 'They're not close, like, but Dave's a solid chap for a time like this, and he can spare the hours, seeing as he's not at work for a week or two.'

'And he's okay with it?'

Jim nodded. 'He can talk, can Dave,' he said. 'About shooting mainly, and rugby, and his little Scotty dog, who's with him as well, so that's a decent distraction. Nowt that George is into, like, but it'll keep his mind off things.'

Harry looked again at the board. It was neat, well laid out, but so far scant on information. 'We heard anything else from the CSI bunch?'

'Not a thing,' Matt said. 'So, all we know is what we were told last night, which isn't much. That being Martha was bludgeoned to death, no fingerprints, no real evidence or clues to give us an idea who could have done it, not even on her car.'

'Which reminds me,' Harry said, and pulled the phone in its plastic bag from his pocket.

'This from the crime scene?' Matt asked. 'You have been a naughty boy!'

Jenny shook her head, staring at Harry. 'If Sowerby hears about this she'll rip your bollocks off.'

'Whose is it?' Liz asked.

'Found it in Martha's car,' Harry explained, 'but I don't think it's hers because I've seen the phone she carries, and it wasn't this one. I mean, hers was a brick.'

'So, is it Sophie's?' Jenny asked.

'We'll ask her when we find her,' Harry said. 'It's locked anyway. Fingerprint security.'

'We could get a court order to get it unlocked,' Matt said. 'Takes ages though.'

'Exactly,' Harry said, stuffing the phone back in his pocket. 'So, let's just wait for now. And do we have anything on Sophie? She's been gone over twenty-four hours now. And wherever she is, she needs to know about her mum.'

'Nothing,' Matt said. 'We've a couple of uniforms being bussed in to help with some door-to-door, but really, for now, we've done all we can.'

Harry was silent for a moment, his eyes back on the board.

'You don't think there's a link, do you?' Liz asked. 'Seems a bit strange for Sophie to go missing and then her mum to turn up murdered.'

'At the moment, no,' Harry said. 'Because the two things are separate incidents, and this could all just be a horrible coincidence. What about the car seen leaving the crime scene? Any CCTV?'

A chuckle ran its way through the team in front of Harry.

'I'll take that as a no, then,' Harry said. 'Shit it!'

'Haven't got much to go on, have we, Boss?' Jim said.

'I'm not your boss,' Harry replied.

'You're the highest rank here,' Matt said. 'So that kind of makes you it by default.'

Harry wasn't sure at all. Not least because of what he'd read between the lines of what Swift had said the night before. Though surely that was all changed now with what had happened.

Harry slumped down into a chair and pulled out the pie he'd bought from Cockett's. It was absolutely bloody delicious.

'How can we have nothing?' he asked, brushing crumbs away from the corners of his mouth. 'Someone caved Martha's head in with something heavy and blunt, probably a rock, they were most likely seen leaving the crime scene, and none of us here have a clue? Doesn't make sense!'

'Jim said you think George is a suspect,' Matt said. 'Can't see it myself.'

'No, neither can I,' Harry said, 'but we can't rule him out, can we?'

A knock at the door interrupted Harry's voiced frustration.

'I'll get it,' Jenny said and jogged over to the door.

Harry turned in his chair to see Jenny stumble back away from the door as a man pushed past. He was on his feet in a beat and met the man halfway. 'And who the hell are you?'

'This is Richard Askew,' Jenny said. 'And he's leaving, aren't you, Dick?'

The visitor held out his hand and in it was something that Harry had seen all too often before: press ID. '*Westmorland Gazette*,' Richard said. 'Just wondered if there was any chance of an exclusive? You know, about what happened? Up at Semerwater?'

Harry eyed up Richard, taking it all in. The man was tall, needle-thin, with a pinched face and huge eyes. He looked, Harry thought, a little like what would happen if you crossed an owl with a crow, then added a bit of rat in for fun.

'News spreads fast in the dales,' Richard continued. 'Probably a good idea to get the facts out there before the rumours, wouldn't you say?'

Harry glanced to Matt. 'Do you know of anything that happened at Semerwater?'

Matt shook his head. 'Nope, nothing that I've heard of. Jim?'

Jim shrugged. 'All quiet as far as I know. Jenny?'

'No, nothing,' Jenny said. 'Bit of a wasted journey, Dick, sorry about that.'

'But if anything does happen, you'll be the first to know, for sure,' Liz added.

Richard, Harry could tell, was not convinced.

'An ambulance was seen,' Richard stated. 'Police cars. People in white overalls.'

'Really?' Harry said. 'That is strange. Well, if you find anything out, let us know.' He moved over and gently guided Richard back to the door. 'Jenny will see you out.'

Richard protested but it was no good. As soon as he was out of the room, Harry turned to face the others in the room.

'Swift wanted this kept quiet. Clearly, that hasn't happened. So how did this get out?'

'It's the dales,' Jim explained. 'You can't have a bunch of people in white suits walking around and them not be noticed.'

'And Martha's a local,' Liz added. 'All those she works as a carer for, they had to be informed that she wouldn't be with them so that they could make alternative arrangements. People put two and two together.'

'Yeah, I know,' Harry said, 'and they usually end up with thirteen.'

'So, what do you want to do?' Jim asked.

'Looks like we've not got much choice,' Harry said. 'Someone get Swift on the phone. We need to head this off before it runs away with us.'

CHAPTER TWENTY-ONE

HARRY STOOD IN THE MARKET HALL BEHIND Detective Superintendent Swift who was at a lectern, which had been borrowed from the local chapel in Gayle, the village next door to Hawes. It was five-thirty in the afternoon and the hall was a-buzz with journalists. Harry was pretty sure that none of this was what Detective Superintendent Firbank had in mind when she'd sent him north. A wind was blowing in from the marketplace outside and there was the smell of cheap coffee wafting in from a little café area to the left of the main doors as you came in. Swift had decided it was best to try and make the press their friends in all of this, so had the two PCSOs serving up hot drinks. Great use of their skills, Harry thought. It made Harry wonder if the man knew his staff at all or had ever dealt with the press before in his life, and if he had, why he thought that rubbish tea and coffee and a few biscuits would make all the difference.

'Bit exciting, isn't it?' Matt said, leaning over conspiratorially to whisper to Harry.

'No, it bloody well isn't,' Harry grumbled. 'Leeches, the lot of them.'

'What are you going to say?'

'I'm not,' Harry said. 'Swift is. He's top dog for this kind of thing so he can deal with it.'

'You really don't know how this man works at all, do you?' Matt said.

Harry was about to ask what Matt meant by that when Swift called for order.

For the next couple of minutes, journalists shuffled along the rows of seats to sit down, each of them whipping out notepads to jot down notes, and phones to record anything and everything that they could. And he would put money on not one of them giving even the tiniest of damns about the actual people involved in what was going on—the victim, the relatives, the friends, the community. No. Because to them, it was all about the story and that godawful nonsense about how the public had a right to know, which they banded around like it was a superpower or something. And Harry had to wonder if the public did. Because most times the news was just gossip, no matter what the story. Wankers. All of them.

'Right,' Swift said at last, as the last couple of journalists shuffled themselves comfortable, 'shall we be getting on, then?'

Harry reckoned on there being at least forty people in front of them now. Seems the nationals had caught wind of it all and sent a few of their own to mix it up with the local press. As to what they knew he wasn't sure, he just hoped that Swift didn't let on too much. Because if he did, there was every chance that the person responsible for the murder of Martha Hodgson would go to ground, and finding them would become even more difficult. And what about Sophie? This was not how anyone should find out someone they know is dead, and particularly not a teenage girl about her mum. But it looked like there was nothing he could do about that now.

A hand shot into the air. It belonged to a well-dressed woman in the middle of the third row back.

Swift held up a hand, palm out like he was Jesus calming the waters.

'Questions after the statement, please,' he said, then pulled out a small pair of glasses, perched them on his nose, and began to read from a sheet of A4 paper resting on the lectern.

Harry didn't bother listening. He knew what Swift was saying because he'd written it for him. Instead, he was just running things over in his mind, trying to find a loose thread he could pull, something that would give him an idea or at the very least a hint of one as to what had happened and why.

So far, and even though there was no traceable link between the two events, all any of them knew so far was that Sophie had run away and Martha was dead. According to what they'd learned from Martha, Sophie had received a text on Sunday from her boyfriend, which had upset her enough to run away a few days later. Harry had no idea why she'd waited so long and not just gone that same day. That in itself didn't make sense. Then, with Sophie missing, Martha had for some reason driven to Semerwater, possibly to meet someone, and been battered to death. The two things had to be linked, surely, but how?

A voice tugged Harry out of his thoughts. 'What?'

Harry saw Swift staring at him. He had moved away from the lectern a little and was gesturing to it.

'Questions?' Swift said. 'And I believe you are best placed to answer them, DCI Grimm, correct?'

If Harry could have set the man on fire with simply the power of his stare, then Swift would have been a charred mess in moments. Putting Harry on the spot like this had not been discussed. The man was throwing him under the bus, making sure that if anything went wrong on the investigation, then it was the new detective from the south who could take the blame, not him, not any of the local team. A proper Pontius Pilate, Harry thought. All he needed was a bowl of water for his hands.

Matt chanced a look at Harry. 'Told you,' he said. 'He's a weaselly bastard, like.'

Harry stood and walked towards the lectern, and the Paratrooper inside him shuffled to the front, as he pulled his shoulders back, his sole aim to make his presence just threatening enough to put the journalists and Swift on edge. He gripped the lectern with both hands.

'Right,' Harry said. 'Now before we go any further with this circus, know one thing: this is not just a dead woman we're talking about. She was a wife. She was a mother. Her daughter is still missing and we need to bring her home safe. So, questions, then . . .'

Hands shot up. Too many by far, Harry thought, and picked one at random.

'Jack Smith, *Daily Mail*. Do you think the daughter did it?'

'Oh, just bugger off, will you?' Harry said, the words out of his mouth before he'd even realised he'd said them. The shocked looks he was now getting from the press didn't make him stop or reconsider, however. 'Really? That's the best you can do is it, Jack?'

'It happens.'

'Does it, now?' Harry said. 'Teenagers battering their mothers to death is a common occurrence, is it? Well, if that's what it's like where you live, perhaps you should look to moving because it sounds like a terrible and dangerous place to me. Next?'

Jack had his hand in the air once more.

'Put it down or I'll come over and rip it off,' Harry said. 'Next?'

Harry felt a hand on his right arm and saw Swift standing with him. 'The hell are you doing, Grimm?' the man hissed.

'Talking to the press,' Harry said, 'because you don't have the balls to. Next?'

Harry picked another hand. It belonged to a woman with hair pulled tightly back in a bun, designer glasses, and an expensive-looking waterproof jacket. It was the kind designed for the most extreme weather, for mountains, and Harry suspected that it spent most of its life in the boot of her car.

'Do you have any suspects?'

'Yes,' Harry said. 'Loads. And if you wait a moment, I'll just get them out of my pocket for you.'

Harry made a big scene of trying to find something in his pocket, then pulled out his hand. 'Yep, here we are.'

Everyone in the room stared silently at the two fingers he had raised proudly to the journalists.

'Any sensible questions?' Harry asked, dropping his offending hand. 'Go on, give it a go. See how well you can do if you really try.'

Another hand, this from a journalist he recognised. It was Richard Askew.

'What is it, Dick?' Harry asked.

'You're not from around here,' Richard said.

'That's a statement, not a question,' Harry said. 'Not very good at this, are you?'

'And isn't the reason you've been sent here,' Richard continued, 'because you roughed up three suspects, putting a long and detailed investigation at risk of collapse?'

Harry glared at the man. Who the hell had he been speaking to? His own DSup wouldn't have said a word, and even if she'd had to say anything at all, it certainly wouldn't have been to imply what was now out in the open.

'I've been sent here on secondment,' Harry stated.

'Your brother's in prison, correct?' Richard then asked. 'Drugs I believe? Do you have anything to say about that?'

'Yes, I do,' Harry snarled. 'Go anywhere near my brother and this lectern will be finding a new home, if you get my meaning, which I assume you do, right, Dick?'

Swift pushed in front of Harry. 'That's all for now, everyone. Thank you for your time this afternoon. Once we have any further information, we will, of course, endeavour to inform you in due course.'

Harry stepped back, clenching and unclenching his fists. His eyes were on the journalist, Richard Askew, who was staring back at him with a sly smile slapped across his face. All Harry wanted to do right then was walk over to him and slap it right back off again.

Richard's hand was in the air once again.

'No more questions,' Swift said, but the journalist wasn't listening.

'What about the other missing kid?' Askew asked.

Harry stepped forward at this, ignoring the lectern, his shadow leaning itself across the journalists in front of him, a storm cloud ready to break. 'What other kid? What are you talking about?'

'Jonathan Airey,' Richard said, checking his notebook. 'His parents reported him missing an hour or so ago.'

'What's he got to do with anything?' Harry snapped. 'Who the hell is Jonathan Airey?'

'You don't know?' Richard said. 'Oh, he's Sophie's boyfriend.'

CHAPTER TWENTY-TWO

HARRY WAS BACK IN THE POLICE ROOM AT THE community centre, the rage in him hot and volatile, a volcano of anger close to blowing, Detective Superintendent Swift staring up at him. The rest of the team were standing back against the walls of the room. Everyone was silent.

'And just what in the name of all things unprofessional and career-destroying was that?' Swift asked, prodding Harry in the chest with a small, pudgy finger. 'Have you lost your mind?'

'We've another kid to find,' Harry said. 'That's what's important now. Sir.'

Harry wasn't in the mood for a dressing down, and certainly not from this puffed up pillock in front of him.

'Oh, and you're telling me what's important now, are you?'

'I'm stating the bloody obvious is what I'm doing,' Harry growled. 'We've got one murder and two missing kids now, and unless we get on this sharpish, who knows where it'll end up.'

Swift turned away from Harry, pushing a hand through what little hair he had left. Then he turned around and walked back towards him.

'This is not what I had in mind when I agreed to have you come here for a few months,' Swift said. 'I didn't want trouble. This is the dales. It's quiet here. And now look what we've got! Christ alive, man! What were you thinking in there? What?'

Harry folded his arms across his chest, if only to stop himself from reaching out to strangle the DSup. As for his point about him being there for a few months, it was the first Harry had heard about it. And with the way things were going, he didn't think he was going to even make it a full week.

'You put me on the spot,' Harry said. 'And that's how I deal with journalists. They're vultures, that's all they are. What you should be more bothered about is how any of what's happened so far got out so quickly! And as for what Askew said? How the hell does he know about a missing kid before any of us? That just shouldn't happen! Ever!'

Swift made to speak, but his mouth just sort of gaped open like a fish before he shut it again with a wet snap.

A knock from the door to the room caught Harry's attention and he looked up to see Richard Allen striding in like he owned the place. 'Ah, good, you're all here!'

Harry met the man in the middle of the room. 'I'm afraid you can't just walk in here,' he said. 'We have investigations underway. Can we talk outside?'

Harry gestured to the door, but Richard didn't budge. 'We have a problem,' he said, 'and with you new and keen I fully expect you to be on it, Officer Groom, was it?'

'Grimm,' Harry corrected, looking to the others for help, none coming forward to offer it. 'What's the issue?'

'Well, there's more of them!' Richard said. 'Those protesters on my land! And you need to move them on! Immediately! It is your job, after all.'

Harry couldn't really disagree, he just thought there were better things for the police to do, particularly right now.

'Are they causing a disturbance?' Harry asked. 'How many are there?'

'They're a bloody eyesore for a start,' Richard said, his voice barking out like an angry German Shepherd dog. 'And it's private land they're on. My land!'

'Look, we'll send someone down as soon as we can,' Harry said. 'We just need to get on with what we've got going on, if you catch my meaning.'

'Well, I don't,' Richard said. 'This has been going on for too long as it is. I'm a local and I should be a priority.'

Harry could feel himself growing frustrated. 'You are a priority, we just have other priorities that don't involve people sitting around in tents trying to protect the country-side,' he said. 'Now, unless someone has caused real criminal damage or grievous bodily harm, then you will just have to wait. But we will have someone down. Soon.'

Harry watched as Richard puffed up his chest, ready to say something more, when another voice called for him.

'Harry?' It was Matt and he shuffled across to stand between Harry and Swift.

'What is it, detective?' Swift asked, ignoring the fact that Matt hadn't been speaking to him.

Matt had his phone in his hands. 'Just heard from Gordy,' Matt said, his eyes on Harry. 'She's with Jonathan's parents. Says the lad left a note.'

'Well?' Swift said. 'What did the note say?'

Matt stared at the screen of his phone. 'Gone to help Sophie. Sorry. Back soon, I promise. Jonathan.'

Harry jumped at this. 'And they say he went missing today, right?'

Matt nodded. 'This morning I think, aye.'

'Then you know what this means, don't you? Sophie's okay. She's alive. And she's with Jonathan. Now, all we have to do is find them.'

HARRY WAS ONCE AGAIN in the police Land Rover only this time it was Matt who was driving. They were heading along the A684, the main road through Wensleydale, and Harry was holding the dashboard and the grab strap above the door white-knuckle tight. The blue lights on the vehicle's roof were flashing, so at least there was some warning to those ahead of them that the man at the wheel was a total bloody lunatic.

'You always drive like this?' Harry asked, as Matt threw them into a sharp right bend, over a bridge, and then into a sharp left.

'Not going too fast for you, am I?' Matt said.

The Land Rover was now racing up a hill, chewing its way forwards with a speed Harry was pretty sure it shouldn't have been in any way capable of.

The route, if Harry had been able to relax and take it in, was a beautiful one. And according to the information Matt threw at him as they hammered onwards, an interesting one as well. In fact, Matt seemed to view the whole thing as an excuse to bestow upon Harry enough facts and stories to make any tourist jealous.

From Hawes, they'd headed out past the turnoff to Burtersett, then on and through to the village of Bainbridge. Here, Matt had pointed out the old Roman fort, which zipped past on their left as they swung up and out of the village. Then, after a long climb up out of the valley bottom, they had trundled through Aysgarth, with its famous falls, which according to Matt had been used in the Kevin Costner movie, *Robin Hood, Prince of Thieves*.

'Had a few mates in that as extras' Matt had added. 'Lots of running around in the trees and shouting while Costner got thrown in the water. Bit of a laugh by all accounts.'

Further on, they'd passed a building hidden by trees on the left which Matt had referred to as 'the temple of doom' on account of it 'looking like a temple, and me and my mate loved that Indiana Jones film as kids, so we called it that, like.'

As the road continued, the valley itself widened, stretching out before Harry with its ancient patchwork of dry stone walls. The place seemed almost untouched by progress, he thought, but not in a way that meant the dale itself or its people were trapped in the past, but more that everything about it seemed to be just right. It hadn't changed much over the centuries because it didn't need to. It was a place of bleak, haunting beauty and the people who lived here were happy to keep it that way.

'Right,' Matt said, as he drove them across a river, through a tiny place called Wensley, then along a straight bit of road, 'Leyburn is just ahead. Gordy is still with Jonathan's family so we're meeting her there.'

'Good,' Harry said. 'And the others?'

'Jim and Liz are already working through a list of names and contacts to see if they can find anything out about where Jonathan's gone, if he and Sophie have been seen. Jenny's ahead of us already, not just to have a presence on the streets, but to check around the local shops with their photographs, get them up and about, ask questions. Someone will have seen something, I'm sure. Two kids don't just vanish.'

'You'd be surprised,' Harry said.

'Aye, I would,' Matt said. 'Everyone knows everyone around here. Scratch one, we all bleed, as the saying goes.'

Matt slowed down, taking the Land Rover up a steepish hill and into the town of Leyburn. The market square opened out in front of them and even in early evening, Harry could see that it was a bustling place, with the car park in the centre still busy.

They headed straight through the town, past a 'nice little gun shop', according to Matt, then up a hill, along by the secondary school on the right, before turning left and then eventually pulling over on a road of bungalows.

'Thanks for the lift,' Harry said, peeling his hands away from where they'd been gripping so tight. 'And the guided tour.'

'No bother,' Matt said, climbing out. 'Just up here, I think.'

Harry followed Matt up the road a little until he jogged over to the right and pushed through a gate. The garden was simple, with a bit of lawn and some flowering borders, and a driveway on which was parked a family saloon car.

Matt walked up to the door and was about to knock when it opened, the space filled immediately with DI Haig.

'You survived, then?' She asked, staring at Harry. 'Though to look at you, I'd say barely. Drives like an idiot, doesn't he?'

Harry and Matt entered the house behind Gordy and followed her through to the lounge. Along the way, Harry noticed that the walls were covered in photographs of a boy growing up in a very happy family. And over the years Jonathan had clearly grown into a good-looking lad. There were photos of them doing family stuff, lots of them being in the outdoors, up mountains and on rivers, a couple of others of Jonathan and some friends tied to a tree holding placards showing axes and badly drawn chainsaws crossed out with a big red 'X'. Others showed him playing rugby alongside ones of him in kit, which took Harry back to his army days. There was also one with Jonathan on a suitably off-road looking motorbike, holding L-plates and grinning widely.

In the lounge, Jonathan's parents were sitting on a sofa together, holding hands. Their faces were lined with worry and drained of colour.

'This is Detective Chief Inspector Harry Grimm,' Gordy said, 'and Detective Sergeant Matthew Dinsdale. Harry, Matt? This is Craig and Hannah, Jonathan's parents.'

Craig stood up and reached out his right hand and Harry shook it firmly. He was a tall man, eye to eye with Harry, and strong, judging by the way his clothes hung on him. This was a man who liked to keep fit, probably by throwing a few weights around on a regular basis. His wife, Harry saw, was well dressed, though she remained seated.

'Firstly,' Harry said, after Craig gestured for him to sit down, 'I know that this is a very worrying time for you. I understand DI Haig has told you everything, particularly the sad news about Sophie's mum, Martha.'

'It doesn't seem real,' Hannah said. 'It's awful.'

'Yes, it is,' Harry said, 'which is why it's so important that we find Sophie.'

'You think she's in danger?' Craig asked.

'I think something happened that's scared her,' Harry

explained. 'I don't know if it's linked to what happened to her mother or not, but I do know that we need to get her home. And as we think she may be with Jonathan, then it makes sense to try and think where he might have taken her.'

'Is he in trouble?' Craig asked.

'We just want to find him, find them both, and bring them home,' Harry said. 'We already have everyone working on it, so if there's anything you can tell me, anything you think is important, then please, tell me now.'

'We've told Officer Haig everything we know,' Craig said, and Harry noticed how he squeezed his wife's hand as he spoke. 'Jonathan's a good lad. He's never done anything like this before. It doesn't make any sense.'

'You've some great photos of him,' Harry said. 'He's in the cadets?'

'Yes,' Craig said. 'Loves it. Anything outdoors to be honest. Always heading off hiking and camping when he gets the chance. He's thinking of going career, you know, A-Levels, degree, Sandhurst.'

'Like his dad,' Hannah said, and Harry spotted the look of pride in her eyes as she looked to her husband.

'Royal Green Jackets,' Craig said. 'Good times.'

'Parachute Regiment myself,' Harry said. 'And yes, they were.'

'I did wonder,' Craig said, then raised a finger to his own face, while looking at Harry's. 'IED?'

Harry gave a nod. 'It's an improvement, I promise you.'

With the atmosphere a little more relaxed, Harry asked, 'So there were no warning signs? Changes in behaviour?'

Craig and Hannah both shook their heads. 'We just came home to find that note and him gone. It really doesn't make any sense at all.'

'How long has he been seeing Sophie?' Harry asked.

'About a year I think,' Hannah said through a sniffle. 'They seem to be very happy together, don't they, Love?'

Craig gave a short nod. 'They're both good students. They don't mess around or get in trouble. I mean, yes, there's the usual teenager stuff, but nothing out of the ordinary. Until now.'

'Can you tell me what happened at the weekend?' Harry saw that his question confused Jonathan's parents.

'How do you mean?' Craig asked. 'What about the weekend? What happened?'

'We understand that Sophie received a text message from Jonathan and that she was upset by it,' Harry explained. 'Do you know what it was about?'

Craig and Hannah's faces were blank.

'That can't be right,' Hannah said at last. 'They're happy together. They don't really argue at all. Yes, they've had disagreements, but that's normal, isn't it? Healthy. I honestly don't know what you mean about the weekend.'

'To be more specific, it was Sunday morning,' Harry said.

'Then it absolutely wasn't from Jonathan,' Craig said, 'that much I'm sure about.'

Harry was more than a little surprised to hear this, considering what Martha had told them. 'And why's that? How can you be sure?'

'Because he was playing rugby,' Craig said. 'It wasn't a match because the season doesn't start up again until September, but the team practices every Sunday morning and Wednesday evening. He never misses it.'

'And you're sure he was there? You're positive?'

'Of course, I'm bloody positive!' Craig snapped back. 'Because I was bloody well there watching him!'

CHAPTER TWENTY-THREE

Harry walked up to the Land Rover, kicked one of the tyres, then leant against the side of the vehicle, swearing quietly. Matt and Gordy stood back a bit to let him get it out of his system.

'You alright, Harry?' Matt asked eventually.

Harry stood back up, stretching his back, and staring at the sky. 'No, I'm not alright. Because none of this makes sense, does it? Not a damned thing! It's horseshit nonsense, is what it is. All of it!'

Harry roared then, not at anything in particular, just at anything that happened to be listening. Because the frustration was building inside him and he needed a release.

'You look like you could do with a brew,' Matt said.

'I don't need a brew, I need something that makes some bloody sense, that's what I need!' Harry said, his voice a barely controlled roar of gravel and anger. 'Because right now, nothing does! Nothing at all!'

'Look,' Gordy said, stepping forward, 'it sounds like Jonathan is a good kid, right? So, whatever he's done, wherever he is with Sophie, there's probably nothing dodgy or whatever about it, is there? We just need to find them and that probably won't take long. These aren't street kids by any stretch of the imagination.'

'No, they're not,' Harry said. 'They're bright kids, studious, and now they're missing. Except that doesn't even make sense, does it? Because the original reason we had for Sophie being missing in the first place was because she had a shitty text from her boyfriend! But we now know that isn't what happened! He didn't send her a message, did he? So that's all bollocks as well. And now he's buggered off, apparently to help her! What on earth is going on?'

Harry walked away then, rubbing his eyes hard till he saw stars. Why the hell would two kids run away, particularly two kids like Jonathan and Sophie? They were neither of them tearaways nor constantly in trouble. They were hard workers, Jonathan clearly had drive and ambition and a properly busy social life. As for Sophie, Harry wasn't so sure what she got up to when she wasn't studying, but at least some of that time was spent with her boyfriend, and he was obviously the very opposite of a bad influence. But above all, the one thing which was bothering Harry most was the text on Sunday morning. If it hadn't been from Jonathan, as Martha had assumed, then who had it been from? If it was the reason she'd run away in the first place, then what on earth could it have been about? And if it was all linked to Martha's murder then the sooner they found Sophie and Jonathan the better, for everyone. Because, as Harry knew from experience, if there's one thing that murder often led to, it was more of the same.

Harry's phone rang and he put it to his ear. 'What?'

'You're just naturally rude, aren't you?'

Harry recognised the voice immediately. It was the pathologist, Rebecca Sowerby. 'What is it?' Harry asked. 'Have you found something?'

'The vehicle,' Rebecca said. 'Just a few things to update you on.'

'What about the body? Anything on that?'

'Were you born impatient?'

Harry waited.

'No, not yet, nothing more than you know already, anyway. Just waiting on a couple of things. Anyway, the car . . .'

Harry hadn't a clue what the pathologist could have found because, after his own look around at the vehicle, it hadn't exactly been filled with clues.

'We took a black light to it,' Rebecca said. 'Didn't expect to find much, but you know how it is, sometimes the world just surprises you. Like how I expect to work with professionals and end up with people like you instead.'

'And?'

'We found bodily fluids,' Rebecca said. 'Which probably explains why the car had been wiped: someone didn't want anyone finding out what's been going on in the car. And by wiped, I mean regularly so, as well as last night.'

If the pathologist was suggesting what he thought she was suggesting, then Harry was completely stumped now. 'You mean someone's had sex in it?'

'More than a little I'd say,' Rebecca said. 'At it like rabbits, if you ask me. Antibacterial wipes are all well and good for getting rid of what the eye can see—we found a half-empty packet under the car—and whoever it was had a damned good try, believe me. But as soon as we took the black light to it the car lit up like the Blackpool Illuminations.

And it was everywhere. Quite impressive really. Amazing where it can end up. Oh, and there was some blood as well, belonging to the deceased.'

Harry had absolutely no idea what the Blackpool Illuminations were. 'DNA?'

'Only from the blood, but I doubt what we find will come up on any records, not unless the deceased was spending her free time with the criminal underworld. Which I doubt.'

'Martha and George don't strike me as the backseat bonk kind of people,' Harry said.

'Well, her car disagrees on that one,' Rebecca said.

'You find anything else?'

'A phone charger for a smartphone, but no phone. Some CDs of the most godawful music you've ever heard. Oh, and a box with six bottles of communion wine in the back, along with some oil, probably from a bike. But you'd know all that, wouldn't you, seeing as you'd already gone poking around?'

'What about the prints?'

'Came up blank,' Rebecca said. 'But I'd guess them to be the deceased's husband and daughter.'

'What about the third set?'

'Not a clue.'

Harry fell silent for a moment. He was thinking about what Rebecca had told him, doing his best to not focus on the sexual liaisons which had occurred in the car, trying to find something amongst it all. And then he had it. 'The phone charger,' Harry said.

'What about it?'

Harry wasn't sure yet, but the only thing he could think of was that if it was Sophie's phone that he still had on him in a plastic bag in his pocket then why would it have been there in the first place? Why would Sophie leave it in her mum's car, and even then, why wouldn't she have the charger with her as well? It didn't add up. At all.

'Look, where's the body? Can you send me an address?'

'Why? What's going on? I'm about to finish up for the evening.'

'Well, you'll have to wait,' Harry said, 'because I'm on my way.' Harry hung up before Rebecca even had a chance to say no.

THE MORTUARY WAS AS to be expected, a cold, clinical place of metal with a chill hanging in the air along with the distinct smell of disinfectant doing its best to cover up a myriad of unpleasant smells in the background. Harry didn't want to be there any longer than he had to be. He wasn't someone who held much truck with places being spooky or creepy, but it was pretty much unavoidable when it came to a place designed specifically to house the dead. Graveyards he found to be different. They were peaceful places, and the dead were just that, dead. But in a mortuary, that wasn't always the case, not as such. Because mortuaries held stories which still needed an ending, whispers of things that had happened to the souls now lying in their drawers, bad things most usually, and the reasons behind them had to be found before real, true rest could be had.

Matt hadn't been exactly keen about driving Harry further on that evening, but they'd arrived in good time and without the need for him to drive like a complete lunatic. He'd also kept the running commentary to a bare minimum, instead, giving Harry the joy of the vehicle's stereo system which was only barely loud enough to be heard as a faint hiss above the growl of the engine and the rumble of the tyres.

Rebecca Sowerby was standing at the other side of a body, Martha's right side, which was still covered in a white sheet. The look on her face as she stared at Harry was rich with disdain and dislike, though he noticed that she used this face on Matt as well, so perhaps she just hated everyone. Which was probably why Matt was standing back and staying quiet.

'So, and just because I want to be absolutely crystal clear on this, you removed evidence from the crime scene?'

Harry had the phone in his hand now having just used the charger Rebecca had found in Martha's car to give it a bit of juice.

'No,' he said. 'I found evidence at the scene, bagged it accordingly, then forgot about it due to being distracted by a conversation with your friend Detective Superintendent Swift.'

'That's not even an excuse.'

'I know,' Harry said. 'It's the truth.'

'And that's a lie.' Rebecca held out her hand and Harry handed her the phone. Then she lifted the edge of the white sheet to reveal a pale, grey hand. With the phone screen lit up, she took the thumb of the hand and rested it on the screen.

'Now isn't that interesting?' she said.

And for the first time, Harry felt that at last, they were getting somewhere.

CHAPTER TWENTY-FOUR

'THE LAST CALL WAS MADE WEDNESDAY,' HARRY SAID, wearing disposable rubber gloves now and scrolling through anything he could find on the phone which would be useful. 'To Sophie. As were the other dozen or so calls throughout the day.'

'Probably just trying to get a hold of her,' Matt said. 'Hoping Sophie would pick up. Any photos?'

Harry clicked on a photo file to find, to his surprise, numerous photos of Sophie, all of them of her either working at her desk or holding various certificates of achievement or work she'd received a good grade for. 'Look at these,' Harry said, and showed the screen to Matt and Rebecca, scrolling through the photos.

'That's just weird,' Matt said. 'None of Sophie just being a normal kid? She doesn't look that happy in them, either, does she?'

'And that's all that's on there?' Rebecca asked, for the first time sounding almost human and agreeable.

'Looks that way, yes,' Harry said.

'They're all date stamped, too,' Rebecca said, pointing at the screen.

Harry scrolled through the photos a little more before closing them down and opening the text messages.

'No, wait, go back,' Matt said.

'To the photos?'

'No, the home screen.'

Harry did as Matt asked.

'There,' Matt said, pointing at the screen. 'Open that app, there.'

'What is it?'

'Just open it.'

Harry clicked on the icon Matt had pointed to.

'Well, shit me,' Matt said. 'Would you look at that.'

Harry stared at the screen as Matt flicked through what the app was showing them.

'Location list, call logs, contacts, WhatsApp, social media. This is a tracking app. Spyware, basically.'

'What are you saying?' Harry asked.

'I'm saying,' Matt explained, 'that Martha has an app installed on another phone—Sophie's by the looks of things here—and she's tracking and monitoring her. Not just her calls, but her movements. Every day. Sophie wouldn't be able to keep anything secret from her.'

'Wait,' Harry said, 'does that mean we can use this to track her now?'

Matt had a look at the app again. 'No, I'm afraid not,' he said. 'There's nothing from yesterday after around seven pm. Looks like Sophie's phone's been off ever since.'

Harry thought back to when Martha had pulled her phone out the day before, its age and size, and how she'd claimed she didn't do very well with technology. Seems the exact opposite of that was true judging by what he was holding in his hands.

'So, she would have known what the text message was that Sophie received on Sunday, then?'

'Yes,' Matt said. 'And it'll be in those records as well. Everything Sophie's ever done is probably there.'

Another more insidious thought struck Harry. 'And if Sophie had her phone with her yesterday, then the whole reporting her missing thing was just a lie, wasn't it? Martha knew where she was all along!'

'Shit, yes!' Matt said. 'But then, why report it in the first place?'

Harry handed the phone over to Matt. 'Find the message from Sunday.'

As Matt scrolled through the phone, Rebecca rested the sheet back over Martha's hand then slid her back into darkness.

'Perhaps you can continue this somewhere else?' she asked. 'By which I mean, please leave.'

'Is working with you always this much fun?' Harry asked.

'Sometimes more so,' Rebecca said, and walked to the door, turning the light off as she did.

Harry and Matt jogged over then followed her outside.

'Look, thanks for this,' Harry said, working hard to sow the seeds of cooperation. 'I appreciate it.'

'Lucky me,' Rebecca said, and with that, she turned tail and walked off into her evening.

'She always like that?' Harry asked.

'Don't have much to do with her really,' Matt said. 'Found the message by the way. Sunday morning, right?'

'Yes,' Harry said. 'And?'

'You're not going to believe it.'

'Who, then? Who sent a text message to Sophie?'

Matt lifted his eyes from the screen. 'Steven Hurst,' he said.

'You're having a laugh,' Harry said. 'The BMW-driving pastor? Why would he send Sophie a message?' Then something else occurred to him. 'Actually, what the hell is he doing checking his phone when he's supposed to be leading a service?'

'And there's something else,' Matt said.' His text was a reply.'

'What?'

'Sophie sent him one first.'

HARRY WAS SITTING in the passenger seat of the Land Rover, Matt behind the wheel. The evening was drawing dark now and he could see that it was going to be another night of next to no sleep and high stress. He'd read through the messages again and again, not just the ones between Sophie and the pastor, but others, too, until he'd felt more than a little voyeuristic and stopped. All he'd gathered from the ones between Sophie and Jonathan were that they were very much in love and not the kind of kids to run off together. Neither had she mentioned anything about what had been said between her and this Pastor Hurst to Jonathan, or indeed to anyone else, if the various texts and message app records were to be believed, which Harry was pretty sure they were. He also noticed that Sophie's messages and communications with everyone had come to an abrupt end on Wednesday. Had she realised then that her mum was tracking her and ditched her phone?

'So,' Matt said, his eyes on the road ahead, 'little Sophie

thought her mum was having an affair with the pastor and decided to call him out on it in the middle of a service?'

'Looks that way, yes,' Harry said, still wrestling with the idea that the Martha he'd met could ever be the kind of person who would be into illicit relationships. 'Why else would she send the message "I KNOW" to him?'

Harry's thoughts were that Sophie had sent the message to the pastor during church in the knowledge that even if her mum knew she had sent it, she wouldn't be able to do anything about it, not right away. The pastor had gone to the trouble of replying, dismissing Sophie's accusation immediately. Which would explain why Sophie had then had her outburst and been taken home by her embarrassed parents.

'Why didn't she just ask her mum?' Matt asked. 'Why go to him?'

'No idea,' Harry said.

'So, what are you thinking?'

Harry fell quiet for a moment before speaking then said, 'Sophie thinks the pastor is having an affair with her mum, and judging by what our friendly pathologist found in Martha's car, I think we can safely assume she is correct in that.'

Matt laughed, but it was a humourless sound, and cold. 'Martha and the pastor getting down to it in the back seat. Unbelievable.'

'She decides to challenge him on it, for whatever reason deciding to not ask her mum or tell her dad. Next thing we know, Sophie's run off and Martha reports it to us, despite having a tracker on her daughter's phone which would tell her exactly where she was at any time of the day. Then, later that night, and according to that phone of hers, Martha sends the pastor a text at eleven-thirty, and arranges to meet him at Semerwater.'

'Why would she do that?'

'Maybe they've met there before?' Harry suggested. 'Could be a familiar place. The car was pretty well hidden in the bushes. You could pretty much get up to anything you want to in there and no one would be any the wiser, particularly at night.'

'And so they meet and the pastor kills her? But why? Doesn't make any sense. Murder's not the kind of thing I'd usually pin on a church leader.'

'Takes all sorts to make a world,' Harry said. 'Unfortunately.'

Harry couldn't believe it himself, but it was what joined the dots, no matter how faint the line. Or, as old Mr Holmes would have sort of said, when the impossible was eliminated, whatever remained, no matter how improbable, was the truth.

'I still can't believe it,' Matt muttered.

'You'd be amazed at what some people will do to maintain the status quo,' Harry said. 'An argument goes too far, one side doesn't back down, the other side lashes out, and before you know it, one person's dead and the other is in massively deep shit. And in this case, we've got a kid who's found out about what's been going on and perhaps the message from Sophie spooked him, he tried to finish it and Martha refused, there was an argument and, well, there we go.' He then leaned forward to stare out the window, at the grey hills around them slipping into shadow. 'How long till we get there?'

'Fifteen minutes,' Matt said. 'And you don't want to call ahead, just in case?'

'No,' Harry said. 'Something like this always works better if you go in with a bit of surprise.'

It was twenty minutes later when they arrived, courtesy of a couple of tractors and some road works.

Matt pointed. 'Leyburn's ahead.'

A few hundred metres or so later, they drove past a petrol station then pulled up on the right beside an imposing row of Victorian terrace houses, with iron railings and grass gardens to the front.

'Lives in the old vicarage,' Matt said. 'Church of England sold it because it was too expensive to maintain and anyway, most vicars seem to be older and on their own, so knocking about in a three-storey, five-bedroom house just doesn't make sense.'

'And this new pastor, Steven Hurst, bought it?'

'Wasn't always a pastor,' Matt said. 'I think he's had a few of his own businesses. He's not short of a few bob, let's put it that way.'

Harry opened the passenger door and climbed out. 'Which one is it?'

Matt pointed over at one of the houses. 'Away then,' he said. 'Let's go and see what he's got to say for himself.'

When they came to stand at the front door, for a moment Harry found himself wondering if what they were doing or about to do was entirely sensible. If the pastor was responsible for Martha's death, then he was a violent man. Very violent, actually, judging by what had been done to Martha's head and face. There was no telling what he might do if cornered. But on the other hand, he wanted this finished as soon as possible, and if he could make an arrest tonight, all the better.

Matt reached a finger up to the doorbell and pressed. Harry heard footsteps approach, then a voice.

'And about time, too,' the voice said, sounding a little irritated. 'I've been waiting for over an hour and I'm starving!'

Matt glanced over at Harry. 'Actually, the Chinese in town is pretty good, though I'm still a fish and chips man, if I'm honest. And if you ask for scraps as extra? Lush!'

The door opened.

For a moment Pastor Steven Hurst's face was one of baffled bemusement. Then it crumbled away to reveal blind panic. 'Oh Jesus, no!'

And the door slammed shut.

CHAPTER TWENTY-FIVE

'Bastard!' Harry yelled, hoofing his left foot at the door, but it didn't budge. He went in at it again, really putting his weight behind it, but all that did was rattle it in its massive hinges and send pins and needles up Harry's leg.

'Round the back!' Matt shouted and raced back down the path to the road and turned right, up towards town. 'Lane just ahead. Take that. The houses have backyards and parking places!'

Harry was on Matt's heels, the sound of their feet pounding the pavement bouncing back at them from the front of the terrace. They sped round into the lane then up to the rear of the houses.

'Which one is it?' Harry asked.

His answer came not from Matt but from the sound of someone sprinting further down the lane in the darkness ahead.

Harry sucked in a breath and dug deep. Running really wasn't his thing anymore, not that it was something he had ever really enjoyed, but seen more as a necessity. And you had to be able to run if you wanted to be in the Parachute Regiment. But he could still move if he needed to, not just because there was still a latent fitness in him which refused to die, no matter how much junk he ate and booze he drank, but also because he was a stubborn arse, and could easily push himself to the point of throwing up and out the other side.

His heart thumping hard now, Harry charged past Matt and onwards into the darkness ahead. He knew he could shout, 'Police! Stop!' but all that would do was absolutely nothing. It had never worked once in his whole life so he wasn't about to give it a try now. And with someone as guilty as this pastor fellow clearly was, judging by the way he had responded to seeing him and Matt at the door, then all it would do would panic him further.

A clatter of bins and a grunt followed by a lot of swearing echoed down the lane and Harry raced towards it, taking a left at the end of the lane down a track beside a wooden garage.

Harry could see a figure ahead now, barely running at all, as it made its way across a sizable garden towards the imposing shape of a large house.

The figure suddenly took a sharp right, like it was trying to dodge back around Harry, but Harry was having none of it and cut him off before he could go any further.

With a leap that Harry was very surprised he even had inside him, he landed on the figure, taking him to the ground with the worst kind of rugby tackle, crushing him with the sound of pain and expelled air.

'Get off me, you mad bastard! Get off me!'

Harry wasn't about to do anything of the sort.

'Steven Hurst,' Harry began, 'I am arresting you on suspicion of the murder of Martha Hodgson.'

'I didn't do it! I didn't bloody do it, do you hear? Get off me! Get off me! Jesus Christ! I loved her, you hear? I loved her!'

Harry ignored the protestations from the body beneath him, more than a little surprised to hear such language from a supposed man of God. But then, if he was capable of a particularly brutal murder, a bit of swearing was nothing, really, was it? 'You do not have to say anything, but it may harm your defence if you do not mention when questioned something which you later rely on in court.'

'Are you deaf? It wasn't me! I found her like that! It wasn't me! Why would I kill someone I loved? Why?'

'And anything you do say may be given in evidence.'

'It! Wasn't! Me! Just listen to me, will you?'

'You okay down there, Harry?'

Harry saw Matt's feet in front of him then stared upwards to see the Yorkshire man doing his best to keep a straight face.

'Don't suppose you've got any handcuffs with you, detective?' Harry asked.

The pastor squirmed, but his verbal tirade had abated, at least for the moment.

'Aye, here you go.'

Harry grabbed the cuffs from the detective then wriggled himself up into a sitting position across the pastor's back, snapping the cuffs on as quickly as possible. He then slumped back onto the grass.

'Wasn't expecting that, to be honest,' Harry said, sucking in deep breaths. 'Quite the workout.'

'It wasn't me! It wasn't! Why would I kill her? I loved her! More than that pathetic bastard George ever could!'

Pastor Hurst had obviously decided to start complaining again and Harry pushed himself to his feet before speaking.

'Well, you're not helping your cause by running away, now are you? Come on.'

Harry, with Matt's aid, helped the pastor to his feet. As they led him back out the way they'd come in, Harry could see that the man wasn't just muddy, but fairly emotional, too. Tears were streaming down his grubby face and he was stooping now, dejected and broken. His posh shirt was a mess of grass and sweat stains. Also, he wasn't wearing any shoes.

'You can't just arrest me,' the pastor said, his voice calmer now. 'You can't. I didn't do it. I didn't do anything! I really didn't. I wouldn't. I just never would.'

'Did you hear what I said earlier, the bit about anything you say now being used in evidence?' Harry asked.

'I don't care! It wasn't me! I didn't do it!'

And then the tears really started.

At the Land Rover, Harry looked to Matt and said, 'Best get him into custody, then.'

Matt's face was one of tiredness and resignation. 'You know what that means, right?'

Harry shrugged. 'More shit mugs of tea?'

Matt shook his head. 'Wensleydale doesn't have any custody suites, not anymore. All part of some cost-saving bullshit or something.'

Harry couldn't believe what he was hearing. 'What? None? Not even one cell?'

'Nope, not a single one,' Matt said. 'So, we have to take

his sorry arse to Harrogate. And that's an hour away from here.'

'Oh God, oh no, what have I done . . .?' the pastor whimpered.

Harry ignored him. 'But we can't do that,' he said. 'It's getting on as it is.'

'That it is,' Matt agreed. 'Not much choice though really, have we?'

Harry glared at the man in cuffs between them. 'No,' he said. 'It doesn't look like we have.'

CHAPTER TWENTY-SIX

It was getting on for midnight by the time Harry and Matt had finally managed to sit down with Pastor Hurst in an interview room. The journey had been easy enough, with no delays, and no real complaints from their passenger in the back of the Land Rover, though, when they'd eventually arrived, he'd looked green with travel sickness. The pastor had been booked in and the Harrogate branch's duty solicitor had been called in. There had been some suggestion that the pastor be handed over to officers working in something called the investigation hub, with the apparent aim of 'speeding up justice'. Harry had politely suggested that the best way to speed up justice was to get out of his bastarding way and let him do his job, and if anyone had a problem with that, then they could have the pleasure of calling not only Detective Superintendent Swift, but also Detective Superintendent Firbank. The threat of waking up two DSups in the middle of the night had been more than enough to have them left alone to get on with what came next. Harry'd had a very brief meeting with the solicitor, giving nothing away at all, and then he'd left him to his meeting with the pastor.

Harry was now at a table, with Detective Sergeant Matt Dinsdale at his side, Pastor Steven Hurst directly opposite, and beside him, the somewhat irritated duty solicitor, Mr Robert Clarke. He was dressed in a tuxedo, so had clearly been having a very good time until the call had come in for him to come down to the station.

'Right then,' Harry began, 'first things first, okay, everyone?' He then reached forward and pressed the record button on the recorder sat in the middle of the table. After stating who was in the interview room, he then read out the caution, repeating word for word what he had said to the pastor while wrestling with him back in a dark garden in Leyburn.

'So, we're all understood on all that, I assume?'

The pastor nodded.

'Good,' Harry said. 'Now, let's start from the beginning, shall we?' He turned an eye to Matt. 'Though to be honest, like Detective Sergeant Dinsdale here I'm sure, I don't really know which beginning to go with.'

'What?' the pastor said. 'What are you talking about? I've told you that I didn't kill her! That's all you need to know. I loved her. There is no beginning!'

The duty solicitor hissed at the pastor, but it did no good.

'Don't you hiss at me! I'd never do anything like that! Ever! I'm a pastor! I was Martha's pastor!'

'And pastors make a habit of sleeping with their flock, do they?' Harry asked.

Steven's mouth clamped shut and his eyes did their best to burn holes in Harry, not that Harry cared.

'You do know that's not a get out of jail free card, don't

you?' Harry asked. 'The whole *I'm a pastor* thing? So why don't you just tell me when it was that you first met Mrs Hodgson?' Harry made sure he put the emphasis on the *Mrs*.

'At church,' the pastor said. 'Where else?'

'When, not where,' Matt corrected him. 'Not a good start, is it?'

'No, it's not,' Harry said. 'Not at all.'

'I don't know,' the pastor said. 'Five years ago, maybe? It was when I moved here and took on the leadership role at the church. Yes, so five years ago. Five. Martha's part of the church leadership team, so we saw each other a lot from the off really. And things just snowballed.'

'Snowballed?' Harry said, repeating what the pastor had said. 'You say that as if it was beyond your control. Is that what it was, Steven? Something beyond your control?'

'It was.'

'You lose control often, do you?'

'Pardon?'

'Get frustrated? Angry, perhaps? Lash out, maybe?'

Pastor Hurst clamped his mouth shut.

'So, you decided to have an affair with her as soon as you met her, then, yes?' Harry asked. 'Or was it more of a slow burn kind of thing?'

'Don't think snowballs can burn,' Matt said.

The pastor turned to Matt, frustration etched in lines on his face, his hands clenching and unclenching in front of him. 'It wasn't like that!' he said. 'Nothing like that at all! Her husband, George, well he just didn't appreciate her. He still doesn't. That bastard doesn't know how good he's got it!'

'You don't like him, then? George?'

A sneer broke its way onto the pastor's face and for the

first time his appearance as the hard done by, wrongly accused fell away to be replaced by something a little nastier.

'He's pathetic,' the pastor said. 'Martha needed loving properly. By me! Not him. He's a worm of a man. But that still doesn't mean I'd kill her if I thought someone was going to find out, does it?'

'So, you did have an affair with her, then?' Harry asked. 'Was it that you got bored? Though, I'm not sure that's how love is supposed to work if I'm honest.'

'No, I don't think it does,' Matt agreed.

'That's not what I meant!' the pastor yelled, his face going a soft shade of beetroot. 'You're not listening to me! Why aren't you listening to me?'

'So, you had an affair with her,' Harry said. 'We just need to be clear. On the facts.'

'Yes, I mean, no, not straight away, anyway. The affair I mean.'

'So, it was just a sex thing, then?' Matt asked. 'Secret meetings by moonlight? A quick shag in the back seat of a car? A rough screw down an alleyway? Didn't know that was the kind of behaviour people in your profession got up to.'

'No! None of that!' the pastor shouted, his voice ricocheting around the room. 'We fell in love! She and George, there was no love there. Hadn't been for years!'

'Bonk and a Bible study,' Matt said. 'Sex and the sacrament? It's an interesting way to run a church.'

'I loved her,' the pastor said. 'That's all that matters!'

'So, it wasn't an affair, but it was, and it wasn't a sex thing, but it was,' Harry said. 'And this snowball was actually love.'

'Yes, I think so,' the pastor said. 'Maybe. I don't know!'

Harry leaned in real close now, his stern and disturbingly

scarred face casting a dark shadow across the table. 'So why did you kill her, Steven? That's all I want to know. What drove you to it? To do her in good and proper? Was she going to tell people, was that it?'

'I didn't kill her! Why would I? I'm a Christian! We don't kill people!'

Harry actually laughed.

'It's not funny.'

'I never said it was,' said Harry, ignoring the pastor's protestations, deliberately trying to wind him up now, to make him trip himself up, say something incriminating. 'So why did you bludgeon her to death? Were you afraid that your secret was going to get out? Or had the flame finally died?'

'Probably the sex,' Matt said. 'The snowball fizzled it all out.'

Harry pulled out the phone he'd found in Martha's car. It was in its plastic bag. 'Do you recognise this, Steven?'

The pastor shook his head.

Harry, with a great display of theatrics, pulled on a pair of rubber gloves, then removed the phone from the bag. While he was doing this, Matt proceeded to produce another phone, resting it on the table in front of him.

'You recognise this one, though, don't you?' Matt asked, pointing at the other phone.

The pastor nodded. 'Yes, of course I do. It's mine.'

'Yes, it is,' Harry said, then lifted the pink phone up for everyone to see. 'Very good. Now, let's see what happens if I press on the screen just here . . .'

Harry pressed his finger against the screen and the other phone buzzed.

'Now, isn't that interesting, Detective Sergeant Dinsdale?' Harry said.

'Very,' Matt agreed.

'So what?' the pastor said. 'Martha and I were having an affair! There, I've said it! My career is ruined anyway. But I didn't kill her! I didn't kill her!'

'Martha sent a text to you on Wednesday evening from this phone, asking to meet at Semerwater that night,' Harry said, resting the phone back down on the table. 'And I'm thinking that the reason for this was because of what Sophie had sent to you on Sunday.'

The pastor tried to speak but Harry raised one of his large hands and shushed him.

'So, you headed out to meet her, an argument broke out between you, and you lashed out and knocked her to the ground and then, well, you just got a bit carried away, didn't you? Because that's what happens, doesn't it? You get carried away? Lose control? But smashing her up like that, Steven, you must have been very upset indeed. Were you upset?'

The pastor was crying now, so Harry kept going.

'You couldn't handle the idea that your secret was out, so you put an end to it. You even wiped down the inside of her car, didn't you? To get rid of any evidence. But that didn't work, because we clever police can see things you can't, and the inside of that car tells quite the story, Steven, let me tell you. A pretty sordid one, if I'm honest.'

'I didn't go anywhere near her car.'

'What?'

'I said I didn't go anywhere near her car!'

'Of course, you did,' Harry said. 'You had an argument in the car, she left, and you followed, and you battered her to death. Then you went back, wiped it down, and sodded off out of there sharpish!'

'No, you've got it wrong!'

'Have I?'

'Yes, you have, because Martha wasn't in her car when I arrived! She was already dead!'

'Bollocks!'

'And why would I kill her if there were witnesses, tell me that!'

Harry stopped, glanced at Matt, then back at the pastor. 'What do you mean?'

'There were two people swimming in the lake. I saw them when I went looking for Martha. So why the hell would I kill her if I knew someone would see me do it?'

Harry leaned back in his chair, pushing it up onto its rear legs. 'You were desperate,' he said.

'I was scared!' the pastor said. 'I found Martha laying on the shore, like she'd been just laid there. I slipped and fell in the blood, panicked, and ran back to my car.'

'But she texted you,' Harry said. 'So how could she have done that if she was already dead?'

The pastor stood up then and shouted, 'You tell me, officer! You tell me!'

CHAPTER TWENTY-SEVEN

It was early morning and Harry was back in his room at the Herriot's hotel. Matt had dropped him off at about four a.m. and he'd managed to get a whole two hours of sleep in before his brain had woken him up as confused as it had been when he'd dropped off.

Pastor Steven Hurst was still in custody. He had a motive for the murder, that was for sure, but after his time with him in the interview room, Harry wasn't so sure anymore. Nothing stacked up. For the briefest of moments, he toyed with the idea that Sophie had done it, but that was just insanity. She had no way to get to the lake for a start, and battering her mother to death to the point where her skull was caved in? No, that just didn't strike Harry as the truth. Though, he had to admit, he'd dealt with that level of crazy in other cases before.

Running through everything in his mind, Harry tried to get things into some sense of order. First, Sophie had sent that text to the pastor, the accusation that her mum was having an affair with him, which the pastor had immediately denied. Next, Sophie had run off and her disappearance was reported by Martha, her mum, who, it turned out, knew where she was all along. And that made no sense at all, not yet anyway. Sophie was still missing, as well, which was troubling, and her boyfriend was with her, too, so that was another problem to add to the mix. All they knew was that on Wednesday she'd been in Harrogate, but after that, nothing. They had the local police out doing their best to try and track her down, but Harry knew how much use that could be, which was somewhere between not much and bugger all. Then, late Wednesday night, Martha had turned up dead on the shores of a local lake, her face caved in. Pastor Steven Hurst's presence at the scene of the crime was in no doubt, not least because he admitted it, but he was pretty adamant that he didn't kill her. So, who the hell did? Harry desperately wanted to put money on it being the pastor, but there was something still niggling at the back of his mind, and he just couldn't work out what it was. And to add to his pain, he was starving, and breakfast wouldn't be served for another hour.

With a yawn large enough to suck in the wardrobe standing opposite where he was sitting on his bed, Harry stood up, stretched, and decided that the best course of action was to go for a walk, if only to clear his head. So, he left his room and headed outside.

Outside, Harry stared at what was left of the dawn. It was a thing of bright gold breaking on the horizon, dashed with flecks of red, and what cloud there was in the sky hung high and faint, candyfloss caught in the ether.

Instead of walking into town, Harry decided to follow the route Dave Calvert had suggested, which took him up left from Herriot's and away from the road, then along a thin path and eventually over a stone stile into open fields. Ahead of him, the path stretched on. It was laid with aged, weathered flagstones and Harry wondered just how many years it had seen in its life, how many people treading its way.

The air was sweet, Harry noticed. There was the hint of something animal in it, no doubt from the sheep in the fields he was now walking through, but there was a richness beyond that, as though the very land itself was breathing out with a scent of living things, of the vast greenness which stretched out beyond the village and to the hills.

Harry carried on, over another stile, and another, just walking, not thinking, his mind a blank. It was as though he was meditating, the events of the past few days not so much forgotten as just allowed to settle for a while.

To his left, Harry saw that the fields sloped downwards to the river and he walked down to it. Grey stone stared back at him, scalloped and carved by thousands of years of erosion from the water it bore. A number of sheep were stood just away from him, further up the stream, drinking water.

Harry could see why people fell in love with a place like this. It was hauntingly beautiful, a landscape unchanged, rich in history and still abuzz with life. For the briefest of moments, he considered kicking off his shoes and socks and going for a paddle, but then thought the better of it. Paddling wasn't a thing for a grown man to do, was it? Certainly not one in the middle of a murder investigation.

A shrill sound shattered the peace and Harry, with a heavy sigh, pulled his phone from a pocket and answered it. 'Grimm.'

'If ever a name suited someone,' the voice at the other end of the conversation said.

Harry recognised the attitude as much as the voice. 'Sowerby,' he said. 'Bit early, isn't it?'

'And yet, you're up.'

'What do you want?'

'I've some new information,' Rebecca said. 'To be honest, should've had this earlier, but there was a delay. I'll be firing the person responsible.'

Harry had no doubt about that at all.

'So, what have you got?'

'The deceased, well she was definitely killed at the lake,' Rebecca said. 'We found the rock that was used. No prints on it, because it had been washed down with water from the lake.'

'How does that help me at all?'

'It doesn't,' Rebecca said, 'but this next bit might.'

Harry said nothing, just waited for Rebecca to say what she had to say.

'The injuries sustained, well they weren't all done at the lake.'

'What?'

'There was an initial blow to the skull, sometime earlier we think. Enough to crack her skull, knock her unconscious.'

'But her car was at the lake! She drove there!'

'I don't see how,' Rebecca said. 'She would've been unconscious from that first strike. And anyway, we found some fragments of varnished wood in the wound, so whatever she was struck with first, it certainly wasn't a rock.'

Harry, for once, was lost for something to say. What the hell did any of this mean?

'You still there?'

'Yes,' Harry said. 'So, let me get this straight. You're saying she was hit on the head with something wooden, knocked unconscious, and then somehow ends up at the lake in her car before being killed with a rock?'

'Either hit on the head or fell or was thrown against something, yes.'

'But how?' Harry asked.

'You're the detective,' Rebecca said. 'I'm just telling you what we found.'

'Anything else?'

'No.'

Harry ended the conversation and was close to lobbing his phone into the water bubbling along at his feet. What the pathologist had told him just didn't stack up. The evidence said that Martha drove to the lake to meet with the pastor. And yet, at the same time, she was apparently injured enough to be unconscious. So, what the hell had actually happened? How did any of it tie together? Had he clobbered her one first, before heading off to Semerwater to finish her off? That made no sense at all.

Harry roared then, loud and angry, his voice shattering the peace and sending the nearby sheep scattering.

He checked the time. It was just gone eight. He needed more brains on this because right now, his was close to short-circuiting.

Harry lifted his phone again and clicked a number from his call list.

'Harry?'

'Jim,' Harry replied. 'Any chance you can get the team together at the community office? I'm heading there now.'

'Sure,' Jim said. 'What's up?'

'Everything,' Harry said. 'Every damned thing is up, and I need help in pinning it all down.'

CHAPTER TWENTY-EIGHT

HARRY WAS IN THE POLICE ROOM AT THE COMMUNITY centre and was more than a little impressed with what he saw in front of him. The whole team had turned up, with Jim being first, arriving just a minute or two after Harry himself, to let them both into the building just before eight-thirty. Jim had then immediately nipped out for 'supplies' and returned fifteen minutes later with yet more of Cockett's cake, along with a decent selection of other goodies, including sausage rolls and apple turnovers. He'd also handed Harry an individual paper bag, inside of which he found a bacon and sausage bap.

'You said you missed breakfast,' Jim had said, as Harry had warmed his hands on the bag. 'Can't have that.'

With everyone now in the room, Harry gathered them around the board set up to initially cover Sophie's disappearance, but which now covered both that and the murder of her mum.

'Thanks for all coming,' Harry said. 'I'll try not to think about what speed you all did to get here in time.'

'So, what've we got?' Gordy asked.

'To be honest, I'm not sure,' Harry said. 'Which is why I've got you all here. So, we can run through it all together and see if we can work out what's what. Because right now, all I can see is that the pastor did it, even though that doesn't stack up now, not after what I was told an hour ago.'

'Which was?' Gordy asked.

'We'll get to that,' Harry said. 'So, from the top.' He looked over to Jim. 'How's about you start us with Sophie?'

Jim stood up in front of the board. Sophie's picture was stuck to it, with various notes around it, covering everything that was known so far.

'Sunday last, Sophie sent a text message to the pastor, Steven Hurst,' Jim said, flipping open his PNB and glancing down at it now and again as he spoke. 'We think she suspected that he was having an affair with her mum and wanted to call him out on it.'

'Why didn't she just ask her mum?' DC Coates asked. 'That's what I'd have done.'

'We don't know,' Jim said. 'And probably won't until we find her, or she comes home.'

'No word then?' Jenny asked.

'Not a dicky,' Matt said, chipping in.

'There was a big hoo-hah at the church because of the reply Sophie received from the pastor,' Jim said, 'which was basically him denying it. The following day, she was in trouble at school, then on Wednesday, she did a runner, taking the school bus, but then heading off to Harrogate.'

'Shopping, probably,' Gordy said. 'Retail therapy.'

'We've found out since that there were sightings of her in the shops in the town centre, and we've got some stuff from

CCTV, but then we've got nothing from the evening onwards.'

'Could she have done it?' Gordy asked. 'Her mum, I mean? Just because the family seem fine on the outside, doesn't mean that they are. Who's to say she didn't just flip out?'

'Why would they be at Semerwater?' Harry asked. 'And where would Sophie have gone that night?'

Matt asked, 'George got anything to say about what happened?'

'He says he had no idea that Martha had even left the house,' Harry said. 'They sleep in separate rooms and she's always up and away before him in the morning anyway, to go to work.'

'Separate bedrooms?' Liz said. 'Really?'

'The only thing we have to add to Sophie's story,' Jim said, 'is that we have reason to believe her boyfriend joined her at some point on Thursday.'

'And after speaking to his parents,' Gordy added, 'I feel a little more confident that Sophie will turn up safe and sound. That lad is a safe bet.'

Harry took a sip from his mug, rolling the information around in his mind. 'So that brings us to Martha, Sophie's mum,' he said and stood up.

'You want a bit of cake?' Matt asked, reaching over with a plate piled high with slices of the stuff.

Harry held out a hand. 'No, I'm good for the moment, thanks.'

Matt shrugged and took a piece for himself before handing the plate to Jim, who then passed it along to the others.

'Martha reported Sophie missing, mid-afternoon,

Wednesday,' Harry said. 'We also now know that despite leading us to believe she had only one phone, she had two, one being an old thing the size of a brick, the other being a smartphone loaded with a tracking app.'

'So, she knew where Sophie was all along?' Liz said. 'Then why report it?'

'Haven't the faintest idea,' Harry said. 'Pretty odd behaviour if you ask me. Anyway, Jim and I had a look around the house and I met George. Nothing jumped out at us there either, mainly because the house was so damned clean. After that, the usual procedures were set in motion when someone is reported missing, and we all headed out for the pie and pea supper.'

'Which reminds me,' Jenny said. 'Need to get you to Cunningham's to buy some running shoes.'

Harry decided to ignore Jenny's comment and continue with the loose timeline of events from the past few days. 'That evening, Martha arrives at Semerwater, her car parked in the bushes. She sends a text to pastor Hurst. He arrives. We received a call from two wild swimmers that her body has been found.'

'So, the pastor did it, then,' Gordy said. 'He's got motive.'

'Except,' Harry said, 'that we now know from the pathologist that Martha was injured before arriving at the lake and potentially unconscious. So, there's no way she could have sent that text.'

'And we're back to Sophie doing it,' Gordy said. 'She arranges to meet her mum at the lake for whatever reason. They argue. They fall out. The argument gets physical. Martha gets knocked to the ground. Sophie runs off and her boyfriend gets hooked into helping her go to ground.'

'The woman's head was stove-in,' Harry said, then

jabbed a finger at Sophie's photograph on the board. 'And I just can't see this girl doing that to her mother.'

'What if our friendly pathologist is wrong about Martha being injured first and unconscious at the time the text was sent?' Matt asked.

'Feel free to challenge her on that,' Harry said. 'Anyway, I doubt that she is. Which means we have two missing teenagers, a murder victim, and a potential suspect, but no way for the murder victim to have either driven to the lake in the first place, or even sent the text message to the suspect to get him to meet her there.'

'How's George holding up?' Liz asked. 'He's always seemed so dependent on Martha.'

'As well as can be expected,' Harry said, 'for someone with a missing daughter and a murdered wife.'

For a few minutes, the team sat in silence, staring at the board, at each other, at the floor, eating more cake, pouring more tea. Harry took the opportunity to stretch his legs, so he headed outside to breathe in some fresh air and hopefully some new ideas. When he headed back in to see the rest of the team, everyone snapped their eyes around at him.

'What?' Harry asked, immediately suspicious. 'What's happened?'

Matt raised a hand. 'Just heard from Harrogate,' he said. 'Seems the pastor has enough money to bag himself a decent solicitor.'

'So what?' Harry said.

'So, he's just been let out on bail. Sorry, Boss.'

'Bloody hell!' Harry shouted then, spitting the words across the room. 'Bail? Really? How the holy hell is that even possible?'

'Like I said,' Matt said, 'he's got the money.'

Harry was fuming. The man was a suspect and now he was out? The hell was wrong with the world? He rather fancied meeting this solicitor and giving him a piece of his mind, a piece which could only be delivered with a hard fist to the skull.

For a minute or two no one spoke, until Gordy stood up to look at the board and broke the silence.

'Not much to go on, really, is there?' she said. 'And what's all these other photos anyway? Can't see any of it being relevant, can you?'

Harry didn't even bother to look at what Gordy was talking about. This whole case was making his head hurt. And with the recent news about the pastor, he didn't even know where to begin with any of it.

'And the crime scene hasn't really given up much, has it?' she added. 'Unless, of course, you count a lollipop stick, a bicycle clip, and a can of iced coffee as murder weapons. The vodka bottle would work though. You can easily batter someone with one of those. Not that I've tried, mind.'

Harry was in the process of stuffing an apple turnover into his face, the cream leaking out of the sides and onto his hands when something about what Gordy had said caught in his mind. He turned around to stare at the board.

'You okay, Harry?' Jim asked.

Harry shushed him with a sticky, cream-covered finger. What was it that he couldn't see? What was it that Gordy had said that had snagged him? He continued to stare, at the photo of Sophie at her desk, Martha's car stuffed into the bushes, with its box of wine and the oil stain and thankfully invisible bodily fluids, the lollipop stick, and the bicycle clip. He thought about the affair between Martha and the pastor, Sophie running away, the boyfriend joining her the day after she'd headed off, the day after her mum had been blud-geoned to death, the photos of the boyfriend on the walls of his home.

'Oh no. . .'

Everyone in the room fell silent and turned to Harry.

'Harry?' Jim asked. 'You okay?'

Harry looked to Jim. 'Land Rover,' he said. 'Now!'

CHAPTER TWENTY-NINE

Harry found George in his back garden. He was busy pruning some rose bushes. Well, Harry guessed that they were roses. They were flowers in a bush sort of thing so that's all he had on that.

'Hello, George,' Harry called over. 'Have you got a minute?'

George turned and on seeing Harry and Jim standing at the side gate he waved at them with his pruning shears and started to walk over.

'Why are we here, Harry?' Jim asked. 'You think Sophie did it, don't you? And that George knows where she is?"

'Just need to have a little chat with him,' Harry said. 'That's all.'

George slipped through the gate and Harry saw worry etched into his face, lines of tiredness reaching out from his sunken eyes. 'Have you found Sophie? Please tell me that you have! She needs to come home!'

'You mind if we go inside for a few minutes, George?' Harry asked. 'If you're not too busy?'

'Can't you just tell me? Please! Where is she? Where's Sophie?'

Harry followed on behind George, with Jim at his heels, and soon they were all inside the house and sitting in the lounge.

The day was turning bright again, and sunlight flooded the lounge, throwing a bright blanket of warmth across the carpet. Jim made tea and brought it through.

'Please tell me Sophie's okay,' George said, as Harry reached for his mug of tea. 'She is, isn't she? She has to be!'

Harry pulled out his phone and placed it on the coffee table. 'Okay if I record our conversation, George?'

'Yes, of course, it is,' George said, snapping a little at Harry.

Harry began recording, and when he spoke again his voice was calm and measured. 'So, George, how long have you known about Martha's affair with the pastor?'

Jim coughed, choking on his tea. 'Harry? What are you on about?'

Harry stilled Jim's protestations with a stern look.

George's already tired face took a darker turn and he sat back in his chair. 'Too long,' he said. 'Too bloody long by far. And to think that they both thought it was a secret! But it's hard to know what to do sometimes, isn't it? You don't want to go picking at something too much in case you end up destroying what you had in the first place.'

Harry ignored his tea. He wasn't thirsty. But he was hungry, though not for food. 'Go on,' he said.

'It was Sophie, really,' George said, leaning forward now, hands clasped. 'I didn't want to ruin her life, upset her when she's so busy with school. It's an important time for her, with GCSEs next year, then A-Levels. The damage something like that could do. Broken homes, broken families. It's not right.'

'So, you kept quiet?'

George nodded slowly. 'What gave it away? That I suspected, I mean?'

Harry thought back over the week. 'Not much,' he admitted. 'It wasn't really anything that you said, more the way you said it. About how you and Martha hadn't slept together for years. I think that was the thing which really hooked me into it, then everything else sort of fell in after.'

Harry saw a smile slip its way smoothly onto George's face, though there was little happiness in it.

'Ah yes,' George said. 'That. I tried to tell myself that it was normal for a very long time.' He laughed then, and the sound was genuine. 'I'm no Lothario, but we all need a little affection now and again, do we not? But she was getting hers alright, in the back of her car.'

Harry was shocked to hear that George knew that as well.

'You seem surprised that I knew about that? I'm not an idiot. She was always cleaning the car. Always. Like I didn't know why.'

George had a point, Harry thought. 'What was Martha like?' he asked. 'Really?'

'How do you mean?' George said.

'Well, the air purifier in Sophie's room,' Harry said. 'The homeopathy medicines—I saw that Sophie had thrown a box of pills away in her room—and the fact that this house is so tidy and perfect. That Sophie's room just doesn't seem like the room of a teenager at all, just a place to sleep and work.'

'You're good,' George said, wagging a finger at Harry.

'The dales would do well to keep you, I think. But yes, Martha, she brought her work home with her, I think that would be the best way to put it.'

'She's a carer,' Jim said. 'What did she bring home with her?'

'Exactly that,' George said. 'Caring. All the bloody time. Too much. About everything. About nothing. Homeopathy was an obsession. Everything had a reason or a syndrome or a condition and it could be cured or dealt with by a new pill or a drop or whatever. It was all just so exhausting.'

'Are you saying she made you ill?' Harry asked.

'I don't think it was intentional, I really don't,' George said, 'but it was still hell to live with. Her constantly fussing, constantly cleaning, bleaching everything. Poor little Sophie. It wasn't fair on her, but I just didn't know what to do. I really didn't.'

Harry saw that Jim, who had taken his PNB out when George had started talking, had yet to write any notes. 'You okay, Jim?'

Jim nodded. 'This just doesn't sound real,' he said. 'Why would Martha do any of this?'

'It's called Munchausen syndrome by proxy,' George said, then caught Harry's eye. 'Oh, I've known what it was for longer than you could imagine. But you see, at first it wasn't so bad. The medicines were harmless, and Martha was such a natural carer. I just thought she was being a bit too keen to start with. But it did get out of hand.'

Harry knew he had to ask the next question, even though he really didn't want to. 'And that's why you killed her, isn't it, George? Because you finally snapped?'

George shook his head. 'That's not how it happened.'

'Come on, George,' Harry said. 'Your wife had been having an affair for years and you knew about it. She'd turned her home into a hospital from hell, trying to cure things that were in her own mind rather than real, and from what I can tell, putting a lot of pressure on Sophie to basically spend her childhood studying.'

'That's all true, yes,' George said, 'but it's not what happened. Honestly, it really isn't.'

'So, you admit that it was you?' Jim said.

Harry had a growing unease that everything they were being told should have been done so in a proper interview room, but the last thing he was about to do was to bundle George into the Land Rover and drive him to Harrogate. He was relaxed here at home, and perhaps that was why it was all just spilling out of him.

'It wasn't planned, not any of it,' George said. 'But when Martha brought Sophie home, well, that's when everything kind of just happened, really. Yes, that's how it was. Spur of the moment, I suppose.'

Harry leaned forward, resting his elbows on his knees, his hands clenched together. 'What just happened?' he asked.

'I knew all about that other phone,' George began. 'Martha always wanted to make sure Sophie was safe, so that's why she had it. And when Sophie ran off, she decided that it would be best for her to . . . oh, what did she say now? Oh, yes, that was it, '*to be a little scared*'. So, she wouldn't do it again.'

'Sophie had run off before though,' Harry said.

'Rather often, too, actually,' George said. 'Usually just sneaking out, just to get away, to breathe a bit I think.'

'There's a worn bit in the corner of the front lawn,' Harry said, remembering what he'd found there a couple of days ago.

'Yes, she'd nip across there sometimes, just to take off for a while, get away.'

'So why did Martha report it?' Jim asked. 'What was the point of that?'

'To scare Sophie,' George explained. 'Martha wanted her to know just how much trouble she had caused by running away, and telling you, the police, was part of that, you see? She thought that if Sophie had a bad time of it, she would never do it again. Ever. There was some sense in her madness.'

Harry remembered something Martha had said about that when she'd reported Sophie missing. It sent him cold knowing that the woman had done it all just to teach her daughter a lesson. That was properly messed up.

'So how did she bring Sophie home?' Harry asked.

'She tracked her down after you'd visited the house,' George said. 'Then, when Sophie was about to hitch a ride with someone, she made her move and brought her home. There wasn't much Sophie could do at that point. Not right then, anyway.'

'And she brought her straight home?'

'Yes,' George nodded. 'And straight upstairs, to lock her in her room as punishment.'

And here it all begins, Harry thought, with a rising sense of dread.

'So, what happened?' Jim asked. 'With Sophie home? Because as far as I know, she's still missing. With her boyfriend.'

'Sophie stood up for herself,' George said. 'I was so proud actually. Really told her mother what she thought. And the language! Goodness me! I think that was what did it, pushed Martha over the edge. Yes, that was why she hit her.'

George's description of the events was playing out in Harry's mind. It didn't make comfortable viewing.

'Martha hit Sophie?' Harry asked.

'And Sophie hit her back,' George said. 'Really threw herself into it. Martha fell back. She was at the top of the stairs and she stumbled. She reached out for me.'

'And?' Harry prompted.

'And I let her fall,' George said. 'I went to grab her, but I was too late, and she fell. It was quite a tumble. Martha's head smashed into the edge of the bathroom door on the landing and she dropped to the floor like a rock. We were both very shocked by it. Sophie started screaming. And then she just took off! I couldn't stop her! When I got to the front door, there was no sign of her. I've not seen her since.'

Harry remembered something from when he'd come to inform George about Martha's death. 'The marks on your arms. From where Martha tried to grab you?'

'No,' George said, 'they're actually from the garden. Not Martha.'

'Why didn't you take her to hospital?' Jim asked.

'Because I didn't want Sophie getting into trouble,' George said. 'It's really that simple.'

'How does this connect to Semerwater?' Harry asked. 'All this happened at home.'

'Martha was dead,' George said. 'Sophie had run off, probably because she thinks she killed her mum, but she didn't, it was an accident.'

'And yet Martha ended up at Semerwater,' Harry said again. 'Why?'

'She wasn't breathing, she was dead,' George explained. 'There was a dent in her skull. I had no choice! I couldn't let my daughter get put away for murder or manslaughter or whatever, could I? It was self-defence, but who would believe that? I couldn't risk it. I just couldn't! So, I didn't take her to hospital. But I had to do something. I had to!'

Harry was connecting it all himself now and he could hear the panic in George's voice, understanding how the man had lost it and allowed events to take on a life of their own. 'So, you drove her to Semerwater, used her phone to tell Steven to meet her, then made it look like a proper murder. And with him being the last person she had contacted on her phone . . .'

'I tried to kill two birds with one stone,' George said. 'Yes. To protect Sophie. And to get a little bit of revenge on that man!'

'But how did you get back?' Jim asked.

'You've a folding bike in the garage,' Harry said, answering Jim's question. 'I'm assuming you put that in the back and that's where the oil stain we found came from. And you left one of your clips behind.'

'Ah, so that's where it went,' George said. 'I did wonder. It was quite a journey back. I'm not exactly fit.'

Harry could see that Jim still wasn't convinced. 'Something else bothering you?'

'The podcast,' Jim said. 'That was Wednesday night as well.'

'I do have rather a lot of stuff pre-recorded,' George said. 'I usually prefer to do it live, but I was able to pull a few things together before driving over to the lake.'

'Did you really think it would work?' Harry asked.

'I knew Steven would get the blame for it,' George said. 'Oh, I didn't think it would stick, but I thought it might be enough to allow things to settle down for Sophie and me. Wrong though, wasn't I? And now Sophie's gone again.'

'Yes,' Harry said, 'but there's still one thing I don't understand.'

'And what's that?' George asked.

'If you thought Martha was dead, why did you do what you did at the lake? Why the violence?'

Harry noticed George's expression change to one of confusion, his brow furrowing a little.

'What violence? What are you talking about?'

'We found Martha on the shore,' Harry explained. 'Her face had been smashed in with a rock. She was barely recognisable. Why do that, George? What the hell drove you to it? She was your wife!'

'But I didn't!'

'Her face was a mess!' Harry said, really laying it on thick. 'You went at her hard, didn't you? All that anger and frustration bubbling out? Did you enjoy it?'

'No!' George yelled. 'You're wrong! This is wrong! What you're saying, it makes no sense! Martha hit her head! I thought she was dead! I thought she was dead!'

'Well, she wasn't dead, George, and you knew that, didn't you? You finished her off! You lost it because Martha had it coming, didn't she? And she didn't stand a chance!'

'No! You're wrong! That's not what happened! None of it! I took her there, left her there, for that bloody awful pastor to find! And now Sophie's gone! And you haven't found her! I don't know what you're talking about! This isn't right!'

Harry went to say something but then a thought came at him, took hold of his gut, and twisted it hard.

'Dear God . . .'

George was sobbing now, but Harry wasn't thinking about that, his mind was onto something else. Something much, much worse.

'Harry?' Jim asked. 'What's wrong?'

'Steven Hurst,' Harry said. 'Steven bloody Hurst!'

CHAPTER THIRTY

'HE WAS SEEN LEAVING HIS HOUSE AN HOUR AGO,' GORDY said, staring at Harry.

After the revelation from George, that he had simply left Martha at the lake thinking she was dead and in the hope of really messing up the life of pastor Steven Hurst, and hadn't actually smashed her skull in at all, Harry had left Jim with him, and raced back to the community office.

'Well that's no bloody use, is it?' Harry said, still out of breath from the run from the Hodgson's house, and making a mental note to go and pick up his now-fixed car. 'We need to find him! Now!'

'How?' Gordy asked.

'He's in a bright red bloody BMW!' Harry snapped back. 'I'm guessing there aren't that many of them in the dales, are there?'

'No.'

'Exactly! Someone must have seen him! We need to know where he is, where he's heading. I know there's no sodding CCTV, but there's got to be something. Do we know which way he was heading when he left his house?'

'Yes,' Matt said. 'Up dale.'

Harry pulled his already pretty horrifying face into something much worse. 'And what does that actually mean?' he asked. 'What direction is up dale, or down dale for that matter? I'm not from around here, remember?'

'He's heading this way,' Jenny said. 'Up dale is up towards Hawes, down dale is, well, back down towards Leyburn.'

Harry couldn't believe what he was hearing.

'So, let's get this straight then,' he said, 'our key suspect was released on bail by some expensive and all too clever solicitor, right?'

Everyone nodded.

'And we know that he left his house, heading this way, an hour ago, yes?'

Again, everyone nodded.

'Then pastor or not, that's a man with something not exactly Christian on his mind, if you ask me,' Harry said. 'Call Jim! Now!'

Harry was at the door then looked around at the others in the room. 'The hell are you just standing there for? Come on! Move it!'

Outside, as they all ran to the police Land Rover and climbed in.

Liz said, 'There's no answer from Jim. Not a thing. He always picks up.'

Matt was in the driver's seat and kicked the engine into life. 'Hold on!'

The tyres squealed as Matt hurled the vehicle out of the

parking area in front of the Black Bull and raced down the hill leading out of the marketplace.

'You don't think he's going to do anything stupid, do you?' Matt asked, his foot to the floor and the engine complaining loudly. 'He's a pastor!'

'I don't care if he's the Archbishop of sodding Canterbury!' Harry roared. 'All I know is that the bastard was having an affair with Martha and probably hasn't taken to kindly to George trying to fix him up for a murder which, it turns out, he actually in the end committed!'

'Doesn't make sense though,' Matt said. 'Why kill her at all? What the hell was he thinking?'

'I don't think he was or is,' Harry said, as Matt heaved the steering wheel hard right, to take them across the road and up the Hodgson's drive. 'The only thing he's thinking of is payback. His affair has been found out, the apparent love of his life is dead, and the husband tried to fix him up for her death which, in the end, turns out he was responsible for anyway. So, this is someone who's life is in absolute ruins as it is. This is not a man with a plan, Matt, of that you can be sure.'

Harry was out of the Land Rover before it had even come to a hard stop, skipping forward as he hit the still-moving ground. Running across the drive he found the front door open and ran through the porch into the house.

'Jim? George? Where the hell are you? Jim!'

The house was silent. Not a sound.

The sound of footfalls announced the arrival of the rest of the team.

'Search the house,' Harry ordered. 'Now!'

The team split up and Harry raced upstairs only to be stopped dead by a call from below.

'In here! Quick!'

Harry was back downstairs and through to the lounge. Liz and Matt were lifting a dazed and bloodied Jim from off the floor.

'He's okay,' Matt said, guiding Jim to sit in on the sofa.

'George?' Harry asked.

'Here,' Gordy said, but Harry couldn't see her. So he followed the sound of her voice and found her and Jenny on their knees beside George, who was flat out on the floor.

'Blunt force trauma to the head,' Jenny said. 'But he's breathing.'

Gordy was already on the phone calling an ambulance.

'Harry . . .'

It was Jim and Harry ducked back to check on him.

'Jim? What happened? Did Hurst do this? The pastor?'

'He just barged in,' Jim said. 'Twatted me something awful over my head with I don't know what. I went down. When I came to, George was on the ground, that pastor was standing over him, and then Sophie turned up.'

'Sophie?' Harry exclaimed, not believing what he was hearing, 'She was here? When? Why?'

'Just a few minutes ago,' Jim said. 'I think she just wanted to come home, to her dad, you know? And she walked in and found that bastard pastor trying to kill him!'

'Where is she now?'

Jim shrugged. 'She bolted. I heard a motorbike though. And the pastor raced off after her.'

Harry was stunned. One murder was something to be dealing with, but this was rapidly spiralling out of control. With Jim attacked, George in urgent need of hospital care, and now Sophie being chased down, Harry found it hard to believe that he wasn't actually back in Bristol and not in Wensleydale at all.

Harry was on his feet and at the door when he turned to the others in the room. 'Where would they go, Sophie and Jonathan? They're being chased and they're on an off-road bike, so where the hell would they go? Come on! Ideas! You know this place and I don't! Think!'

'Off-road,' Jim said. 'Where that bastard can't follow them in a BMW.'

'The Roman Road,' Liz said. 'That's where I'd go. He'd only get so far chasing them up there before his car came a cropper.'

Harry snapped his eyes to Matt. 'Keys! Now!'

'They're still in,' Matt said.

'Cuffs?'

Matt lobbed him his own and Harry was gone before anyone could jump up to join him.

The Land Rover coughed to life and Harry spun it around in the drive and turned right, pointing the vehicle up the road. He floored it, though the Land Rover didn't exactly respond immediately, and to Harry, it didn't feel so much that the vehicle got faster as gained momentum.

At the right turn to Burtersett, Harry screeched the vehicle off the main road and up into the tiny village, racing through as fast as the Land Rover could take him. Out of the village, zipping by Jim's parents' farm on the left, Harry knew that anything could be happening in front of him. For all he knew, the two kids had fallen off their bike and that bastard pastor was onto them already. The thought was enough for him to drop a gear, kick the accelerator hard, and send the Land Rover screaming forwards.

Harry saw the Roman Road ahead, then swore under his

breath, remembering that it was a crossroads and that they could have gone either left or right, left heading down, right taking them back up into the hills.

Harry went right.

The road was rubble and stone and the Land Rover chewed it up like it was having the best time of its life. Harry on the other hand was not, his head bouncing off the roof of the cab because he was driving too fast. But he had to. He needed to put an end to this and now.

The road took a sudden steep dip, hit a sharp corner, then rose again and it was here that Harry's luck turned. In front of him, smoke pouring from its bonnet, was a red BMW. Harry nearly fist-pumped, but then he saw just ahead, further up the hill, a motorbike on its side, wheels spinning, smoke rising.

The BMW was off the road, but still sticking out too much to let Harry past. But that didn't stop Harry and he barged the police Land Rover into the pastor's car, squeezing past with the sound of ripping metal.

At the motorbike, Harry killed the engine and was out of the vehicle. He looked around and all he could see was hills and moors stretching on before him.

'Sophie!' Harry called out. 'Jonathan! Where the hell are you?'

A scream caught on the wind came to Harry and he turned to it. It came again, gave him a bearing, and he followed it, over the wall running alongside the Roman Road and up onto the fell in front of him.

Harry raced over a rise to find himself stumbling down the other side and into the pastor, shock on his face at the sudden arrival of someone he clearly really didn't want to see. Before Harry had a chance to get to his feet, the pastor hoofed him one hard in the gut. Harry coughed and tasted vomit. Through the tears in his eyes, he saw Sophie just away from him now crouching next to Jonathan, who was bleeding from his mouth.

The pastor came in again, but this time Harry was ready, shifting himself just in time, and the momentum of the kick put the pastor off balance. Harry took the chance and swept his right leg out, catching the pastor behind the knees, felling him like a tree. Then Harry was on top of him, his knees digging hard into the man's back.

'Get off me! Get off me!'

Harry ignored him, yanked his arms behind him, then snapped the cuffs onto his wrists.

'You,' Harry said, rolling off the pastor's back, 'are nicked.'

Harry was breathing hard as he crawled away on all fours from the pastor, who he left busy swearing into the grass. He looked over to Sophie and Jonathan and pushed himself to his feet. Harry could see that they were both terrified.

'I'm from the police,' Harry said. 'It's okay. You're safe now.'

'Are we in trouble?' Jonathan asked.

'Probably,' Harry said. 'But that's why I'm here. To help, okay?'

'My dad,' Sophie said. 'Is he alright?'

'The police are with him,' Harry said. 'They've called an ambulance.'

The boy and the girl didn't move.

Harry held out his hand to the girl. 'Sophie?'

The girl nodded and Harry saw tears starting to brim in her eyes.

'I know what happened,' he said. 'And I know what you think, but you didn't kill your mother, okay? Your dad told me everything that happened. And he needs you now. More than ever. He needs you to come home.'

For a moment no one moved. Then the tears flooded out and Sophie ran to Harry. He caught her. And he wasn't about to let her fall.

CHAPTER THIRTY-ONE

'You're sure about this?'

'I think so.'

'Then you're mad as well as ugly.'

'Thanks.'

Harry stared out across the lake. It was late evening now, the moonlight reaching across the water, an eerie beam of light stretching towards and over him. His feet were in the water, which was a start, and it was properly bloody cold. Jim was standing just away and back a little, holding a towel.

'You remembered the flask of that hot coffee of yours, right?' Harry asked. 'You didn't leave it back at yours?'

'Oh, I remembered it alright,' Jim said. 'Not that it'll do much good, like. You'll be dead in a few minutes anyway. Hypothermia or something. Probably have to drag the lake to find your body.'

Harry stepped forwards up to his ankles. The cold of the water raked at his skin, stabbed knives of ice into him.

'Remind me why I'm doing this?' Harry asked.

'Remind you?' Jim said. 'You've not given a reason yet!

Just said you were off to Semerwater and that you wanted me to bring a towel and a hot drink!'

Harry laughed. And it felt good to do so. It was the weekend after one of the strangest weeks he'd ever had in his life. So it had only seemed fitting that he finish it off doing something which, to him at least, seemed just as strange. And after meeting the two wild swimmers earlier in the week, even though the circumstances hadn't exactly been the best, he'd been intrigued by what they'd done. And now, here he was, about to do the same.

'You don't have to, you know,' Jim said. 'No one knows that you're here. I won't tell, I promise.'

Harry edged further still into the water, up to his knees now. He couldn't feel his feet at all, not even the pebbles that he was standing on.

'You're really going to do this, aren't you?' Jim asked. 'You're mad, you know that, right?'

Harry wondered what his brother would say if he was here now to see him do this, his big, responsible, older brother, throwing himself into a cold, black lake. Would he smile? Would he laugh? Because really, that's what Harry wanted more than anything, to see his younger brother happy.

'Come on,' Jim called out. 'Just get it over and done with! You're almost there!'

He'd bring him here one day, Harry thought to himself, slipping deeper into the water. Yes, that's what he would do. He would find their father, make him pay for what he'd done, then bring Ben here and watch him laugh.

Then, with a roar, which broke into a yelp, Harry threw himself forward and disappeared beneath the waves.

If you enjoyed Harry's gripping introduction to life in the beautiful-but-deadly Yorkshire Dales, then dive straight into the next chilling case in Best Served Cold.

JOIN THE VIP CLUB!

SIGN up for my newsletter today and be first to hear about the next DCI Harry Grimm crime thriller. You'll receive regular updates on the series, plus VIP access to a photo gallery of locations from the books and the chance to win amazing free stuff in some fantastic competitions.

You can also connect with other fans of DCI Grimm and his team by joining The Official DCI Harry Grimm Reader Group.

Enjoyed this book? Then please tell others!

The best thing about reviews is they help people like you: other readers. So, if you can spare a few seconds and leave a review, that would be fantastic. I love hearing what readers think about my books, so you can also email me the link to your review at dciharrygrimm@hotmail.com.

AUTHOR'S NOTE

My two brothers and I grew up in large, draughty houses which came with my dad's job, that being a Methodist minister. A key part of this role was that we had to move house a few times, and I don't mean to another part of the village. In 1981, we moved from Gloucestershire up to Hawes, in Wensleydale. It was quite a culture shock. I still remember leaving our old house, the long journey, pretty much everything about it.

The journey, which had been in a long wheelbase Series 3 Land Rover, had taken most of the day. We arrived in the middle of a rainstorm, exhausted, and probably just a little bit grumpy. I was eight years old at the time, my brothers five and one. I have a feeling that all my parents really wanted to do was get into the house and collapse. However, we were met at the house by the local church leaders, from chapels up and down the dale, who took us through to the kitchen where a meal had been laid out for us. And we had to eat it while they stood around and talked to us. It was a kind gesture, because all they wanted to do was make us feel welcome. It was also so alien to us that the memory is with me even now.

We spent five years in Hawes. And no, they weren't all sunshine and daffodils and running through fields. But Hawes and the dales welcomed us and it became our new home. And a rich and splendid one it was, too.

What can I remember specifically, that made it thus? The list is long. Our first winter there greeted us with snow two feet deep in the garden and across the road. We had a huge vegetable plot in the back garden. Dad bought a few pet lambs, which we kept in the garden, the smell of the powdered milk we had to mix up for them was rich and sweet. The scenery was astonishingly beautiful. Greasy Joe's fish and chip shop in town was the best, not least because of the scraps you could have on the chips. Everyone wore Doc Marten boots and listened to heavy metal. Harvest festivals were absolutely fantastic and my mate Dave would always come along to buy grapes when the food was auctioned off afterwards to raise money. Shooting and fishing were a part of most people's lives, including our own. The youth club was epic. The bus journey down dale to Leyburn school was a mix of people smoking, stopping off on the way back at the sweet shop in Aysgarth, and listening to either Elvis or The Beatles, because they were the only two eight-track tapes that Tommy, the bus driver, owned. There were only two other boys my actual age in the local area. You couldn't move for Land Rovers. Sheep covered the fells and most of the kids I knew seemed to want to become farmers, like their parents. It rained a lot, and after a storm, the water in the house would turn brown. I could go on, but I won't!

So why have I written a crime novel set in this truly magical place? Simple really: I wanted to set it somewhere that I knew and that I loved. And there really is nowhere that I know as well, or love as much, as Wensleydale. It is a wonderful place full of wonderful, friendly people, and throwing Harry Grimm into the middle of it has been the most fun I think I've ever had with writing. And you know what? I cannot wait to find out what happens to him next!

So, finally, thank you for sparing just enough of your valuable, precious time, to join me on the start of what I hope is a wonderful new adventure. The dales are beautiful and I hope that in some small way, as well as giving you a fun little story, I've helped to paint a picture of somewhere you really have to visit. Because you know what? It's not actually grim up north at all, it's beautiful.

Dave

ABOUT DAVID J. GATWARD

David had his first book published when he was 18 and has written extensively for children and young adults. *Grimm Up North* is his first crime novel.

Visit David's website to find out more about him and the DCI Harry Grimm books.

 facebook.com/davidjgatwardauthor

THE DCI HARRY GRIMM SERIES

Welcome to Yorkshire. Where the beer is warm, the scenery beautiful, and the locals have murder on their minds.

Printed in Great Britain
by Amazon